According to
His Purpose

and

Other Short Stories

Christmas Carol Kauffman
Compiled by Marcia Kauffman Clark

DIGITAL
LEGEND

Christmas Carol Kauffman

1901–1969

Christmas Carol Kauffman was born on December 25, 1901, in Elkhart, Indiana, the second daughter of Abraham Rohrer and Selena Bell Wade Miller. Carol, as she was known, graduated from Elkhart High School and attended both Hesston and Goshen Colleges. She began writing short stories at Hesston College and continued writing one short story per month for the *Youth's Christian Companion*. In total, she wrote more than one hundred short stories.

In 1929 she married Nelson Edward Kauffman. They served together at the Hannibal Mission Church in Missouri for twenty-two years, where Nelson was the pastor. They are parents of four children. While in Hannibal, Carol began writing book-length inspirational true stories that were published by Herald Press.

Lucy Winchester, her first book, was published in 1945. Throughout the next two decades she authored six additional books: *Light from Heaven* (1948), *Dannie of Cedar Cliffs* (1950), *Not Regina* (1954), *Hidden Rainbow* (1957), *For One Moment* (1960), and *Search to Belong* (1963). After her death, two more books were published in 1971: *Little Pete and Other Stories*, a collection of thirteen of her short stories, originally written in 1928, and *One Boy's Battle*, written in 1948 and originally titled *Unspoken Love*. All nine of her books continue to be published today.

Christmas Carol Kauffman died on January 30, 1969.

For
Nellie Marie Miller Mann Whitmer
Who typed most, if not all,
of Carol's short stories

Send inquiries to:
Digital Legend Publishing
1994 Forest Bend Dr.
Cottonwood Hts., UT 84121

Visit www.digitalegend.com
or write to info@digitalegend.com
or call toll free: 877-222-1960

Printed in the United States of America
ISBN: 978-1-944200-25-1

Contents

According to His Purpose

By *Christmas Carol Kauffman, age 50, Hannibal, Missouri*
Originally published December 9, 1951, through January 13, 1954,
in *the* Youth's Christian Companion

The day had come. It was perfect, balmy, and warm. The sweet spicy odor of spring's first honeysuckles scented the air of Hempton Falls. The glossy green vines on the white wooden trellises of the college dormitory porch were covered with great patches of blossoms.

Laura Lou came through the open door, crossed the veranda, and hesitated for a moment by the vines. Her brown hair lay in soft waves that were pinned high. Her creamy white gabardine dress, although new, looked as though it had always belonged to her. In one hand she carried a large paper-bound book and a lace-edged handkerchief, with the other she reached up and gently touched a honeysuckle. She was tempted to pick it from the vine, but instead she turned and started down the steps.

She looked to the right, then to the left. People crowded the walks that circled the campus fountain and led to the auditorium. She searched their faces. Maybe he was already in the auditorium. The crowd was gathering. Every seat would soon be taken. Perhaps he had seen how late it was getting and had decided to go on in. He had written that he'd try for a seat near the front.

She could wait no longer. The dormitory was practically empty. Every girl in the chorus had already gone to room C, where the chorus was meeting for final instructions. She waited, watching from her third-floor window until she could wait no longer. Twice she was certain she had seen Edwin's car coming in the west gate entrance—only to be disappointed. Her roommate had reassured her, "You can depend on Edwin, Laura Lou. He is a Christian and you know he loves you. If he isn't here at the time he said, it is because something he hadn't anticipated delayed him. Don't you worry now, dear; he'll come."

"I know," answered Laura Lou softly. Then she turned toward Mamie confidently, gently waving her handkerchief back and forth in front of her slightly flushed face. "He will come yet."

But the hour had come. She had listened for her personal ring for the past sixty minutes. One by one the girls in white had crossed the campus to gather in room C. She did not have time to get out his last letter and reread it. She already knew it from memory. Laura Lou had read it and reread it and folded it and unfolded it, and pressed it between her fingers until the ink was blurred.

"I will see you on the first of June, not later than one o'clock. I will come to the dormitory as soon as I arrive, so we can talk just a little before the chorus program. Be looking for me, my love. I can hardly wait now that my plans are all made."

It had been his suggestions in the first place. He had mentioned in one of his letters early in the spring how he would like to drive out for Laura Lou's commencement and take her home with him.

Laura Lou was thrilled. She was excited when she read the letter, and she answered immediately.

Laura Lou Gentry was not a child. At twenty-two she was dignified, refined, mature, and sure-minded. She liked Edwin Ferdella more than any other young man she had met or dated. It was perfectly agreeable with her, in fact it was the most pleasant thing that could possibly happen, if he would be in the audience when she was granted her degree.

Her mother couldn't come, for she had had a slight stroke six weeks previous and her father would not leave her mother. Laura Lou was disappointed, for her parents had planned to be present for her graduation. Edwin would come and he'd be the most important person in the audience to her.

Laura Lou was thrilled! She'd look her best! She'd sing her best for Edwin.

She'd written about it to her parents, to her married sister in Springfield, to her gentle grandmother who lived with her Uncle Hen in Detroit. In all her letters to Edwin, she had mentioned his coming. She had dreamed about it, practiced for it, planned, prayed, and worked for it for weeks.

Not a detail had she overlooked. Her dress, her shoes, her hair, her fingernails, and everything had been given careful attention. There was not a note, not a pause, not a crescendo, not a hold that she did not know perfectly. She would sing her solo in the cantata for Edwin.

Her heart pounded as she walked swiftly across the campus. People were filing into the auditorium. "Everyone is here now?" inquired the music director. Laura Lou slipped quietly into her place.

From the platform she scanned the sea of faces below and those in the balcony. Once she thought she spotted him, but the same second she knew she had been mistaken. Is Edwin not there? Fresh disappointment gripped her. A mob of questions raced through her mind. It would soon be time for her to sing her solo. The tyranny of fear would rob her of her composure and breath control. She felt sick. What if he had been in an accident! Something must have happened! Surely he would not disappoint her. It had to be anything in the world but that, for they had sealed their engagement on Christmas day. Edwin would have written, telegraphed, or phoned had his plans been altered. At first his employer wasn't going to let him time off. He had asked for only two days. But in the past three weeks, every letter she had received assured her Edwin had been granted his request.

The moment came—that moment she had so diligently practiced for. She must do her best. Could it be that he was in the audience and she had failed to catch his eye? She cleared her throat very, very softly, stepped forward, facing the crowd. Every eye was on her. She drew a deep breath, and lifting her heart to God prayed inaudibly before she signaled the director that she was ready to sing. The chorus of sixty voices hummed the accompaniment. A tall young man with well-groomed chestnut hair, tiptoed in the side door and took a folding chair in the side aisle. Was that Edwin? Her heart skipped a beat. It was not!

Edwin Ferdella leaned over the counter. He turned the watch over in the palm of his hand and looked at it with happy seriousness. Would she like it? He had selected it from the four that he liked best.

"You'll make no mistake in that watch," spoke the gray-haired jeweler with an accomplished, pleasing, business-bred smile. His voice was soft and smooth. "She'll be as pleased to get it as you'll be to give it to her. And, of course, it's guaranteed, and I've been dealing with that company for thirty years. That's the watch I'd get.

"I'll take it."

"Do you want to make a down payment and have it put on—?"

"Oh no sir. I want to take it with me now," and Edwin handed the watch to the jeweler and pulled out his billfold.

For over a year Edwin had worked in Haydren, five miles from Laura Lou's country home. The romance started after a Sunday country jail service in Coberstum Mills. Edwin had gone with a male quartet from his church of their choice in Haydren from their farm in Illinois. Because of his father's weak heart, the doctor had advised a change from strenuous farm work, and because there was a church of their choice in Haydren, the Ferdellas chose to locate there.

Their life was centered in their church. Although Tomas Ferdella held no other office in the church except that of a trustee, he was thoroughly in harmony with its forward evangelical program. He wholeheartedly supported every undertaking. He and Mrs. Ferdella had the love of God on their faces and diligently taught their children precept upon precept from their infancy.

Edwin, the eldest of the three sons, had accepted Christ at the age of eleven, and although he had gone through a number of soul struggles over doubts, at twenty-one he was a victorious Christian, radiant with the glory of Christ's atoning power on his handsome face. Salvation by faith was his personal possession. He was a happy, burning, useful Christian. The church leaders recognized his talents and made use of them. Edwin not only sang a lyric tenor, but he could also speak with conviction in fluent, forceful speech. He taught a class of rollicking teenage boys.

Edwin had watched Laura Lou Gentry with admiring eyes. Her sweet, unobtrusive, sincere manner had attracted him each time their ways had met. He liked her full, fair face, her soft gentle voice and refined speech, but most of all her genuine, conscientious spirit. He had watched with every growing interest her precise attention to church assignments and her personal testimonies in prayer meetings and Bible study classes.

When Edwin Ferdella asked Laura Lou for a date, it was not on the spur of the moment. He was not the kind to seek the admiration of many girls. Although occupied with his work at the corner grocery store, a correspondence course, quartet practices, and his Sunday School class, he had moments when he could not conceal the emptiness deep inside. He longed for Laura Lou's company.

Several girls had very noticeably tried to make themselves appealing to Edwin Ferdella by thrusting themselves before him at every opportunity. But their systems and schemes had failed. Davera Maloney in particular had been determined to win in the game to catch Edwin Ferdella. Her father had hired Edwin and given him above-average wages. Her father and Edwin could someday be partners in business. Why couldn't he see what a chance was his? She had all but mentioned it one Saturday when she had helped in the store. She thought up a thousand and one ways to get him to fall in love with her. They sacked beans together, filled counters together, weighed out sugar together, and whenever she was in the store after school hours or on Saturdays, she would call Edwin to "come do this please," or "come over here Edwin," or "Edwin, Daddy wants you to help me do this" until Edwin decided he'd apply for a job at the dairy. Over and over, his feet wanted to take him in the opposite direction.

"Can't you ever let me coax a smile out of you, Edwin?" whined Davera one evening. "You'd think I was ice," and she looked at him with her big brown eyes.

Davera Maloney seemed like a lifeless vine hanging over the back door of an old house, compared to Laura Lou Gentry. Everything about Laura Lou seemed real, alive, and inspiringly wholesome. He wanted a girl he would have to work for, not one he could have for nothing. The false warmth about Davera made his heart grow icier every time he was around her. Laura Lou's face was spoke warmth and peace and security.

Edwin had confided in his mother and father about his attraction for the Gentry girl. If he lived to be as old as Methuselah, he would never forget how his father's shoulders rose and fell as he drew in a long deep breath and two tears crept slowly from his serious gray eyes when he answered. "Such a step, my son," and his father glanced over to Edwin's mother sitting in her favorite rocker, book in lap, "would surely be of the Lord."

A strange holy silence filled the room. Edwin caught is breath. He bit the inside of his cheek.

"What makes you say that, Father?"

Mr. Ferdella ran both his hands back over his iron gray hair, and when he spoke, his voice was a trifle unsteady, but the words came forth as though they were the most important, the most significant words he had ever spoken to his first-born, as though he had collected, weighed, graded, and polished his answer with eternity in mind.

"We've been praying for this very thing for years, Edwin, Mother and I. She is a jewel."

Mrs. Ferdella smiled and nodded assuredly. Nothing of human connection between Thomas Ferdella and his sons was alien to his deepest interests. Every ambition and prayer for each one was the highest quality. Mr. Ferdella looked at his son with fond love.

And so on a Sunday afternoon at the close of the jail service in Coberstum Mills, Edwin, tall, straight, and handsome, asked Laura Lou Gentry if he could take her home from church that evening.

She looked up into his earnest, manly face with no hint of alarm, took half a step back, and a faint smile played around her pretty lips.

"You may," she answered, trying to hide her emotion. She must not let him guess, she must not even let herself know how joyful it made her feel, especially right there with half a dozen others watching if they wanted to. She walked immediately to Marion Drew's car.

The country road between Coberstum and Haydren was beautiful, but now and then along the way there were rather melancholy looking dwellings which set Laura Lou to thinking. Maybe the folks who lived there were old, or worn, or unhappy, but she vowed that if she were ever mistress of a home, she'd do her share to make it look attractive. She'd not allow old frayed rugs and ragged blankets to be hung over the garden fence; or let big weeds grow in her yard. She lost herself in a dream of a cozy little home.

She yearned with a clean warm feeling for a chance to express her deeply hidden love. Then it began to rain, first in great drops like silver half dollars; then in a steady downpour. It washed all the dust off of Marion's new car. He laughed about it. Marion Drew always laughed and chuckled about anything. Everyone called him happy-go-lucky Drewie. He was always ready to take groups to the county jail or any place else. He was everybody's brother and nobody's boyfriend.

Laura Lou sat in the back seat listening and saying little, but she felt like the rain was washing all the dust from her mind and soul and body. She planned which dress she'd wear; she wondered what they would talk about and how it would feel to sit beside Edwin Ferdella. Her blue eyes became bright. Rain could not spoil her date.

Chapter 2

Edwin left for Hempton Falls at daybreak. By the back window of his car he hung his Sunday suit and in a box on the seat was his freshly laundered white shirt. Beside him was a shoe box containing the lunch his mother had prepared. He wouldn't take time to stop at a restaurant. He planned to reach Hempton Falls in time to see Laura Lou before the program. He'd take the watch out of his pocket present it to her, observe her eyes glow, then slip it onto her wrist.

He hummed all kinds of little tunes, sometimes whistled as he wheeled along, watching the sun come peeking in through the trees along the horizon. He felt strong, happy, and confident—very confident—that no other young man living or dead had ever won so charming a lady. He rehearsed every development of their romantic first ride in the rain to her last letter. "I will be overjoyed to see you, Edwin. Don't disappoint me. I'll be listening for my dormitory ring. It will make me very happy to have all my classmates meet the man I've promised to marry. Yours forever, Laura Lou."

Once he was tempted to stop at a filling station to telephone her that he was halfway there. But why delay his progress? She was undoubtedly busy doing her final packing. In a few more hours they would be seeing each other. The six months of separation had been long, yet short: short because Edwin had held himself industriously to his work, utilizing every spare moment off duty in his basement workshop making furniture for their future home. Not a thing had happened between them during their three years of friendship to mar their happiness. Their friendship had been a steadily uplifting, spiritual experience. He held the car at fifty, enveloped with anticipating and happy visions of sitting in the audience and listening to Laura Lou's part on the program. He remembered with vivid joy her sweet soprano voice quite unlike any other he had ever heard. It was good to be alive. Was any man his age ever happier? Edwin doubted it.

He sped up along the hill before him. The curve at the crest was sharp and, as he turned it carefully, he saw, abruptly to the right, a young woman clutching a tiny child in her arms. Her clothing was ablaze all across her back and shoulders, as she stumbled, screaming, from the back door of a small, one-story frame house, about forty feet from the road. Edwin held his breath, drove into the yard, pulled the emergency brake, jumped out of the car. "My baby! My baby!" screamed the woman frantically. Her voice spoke terror, and her eyes were red and wild.

Edwin ran, pulling off his poplin jacket. He was horrified. He threw his jacket around the woman's burning clothing—trying to smother the flames.

"Take my baby," she cried. "Take her first." Edwin reached for the baby and his scorched jacket dropped to the ground. He brushed his own right sleeve that had ignited in several spots, and took the infant from the mother's blistered arms. He tore away the little blue plaid blanket that was smoking like wet half-dead leaves. The tiny pink doll face, half-buried in the hot blanket, was innocent and sweet. The child was gasping for breath, but did not open its eyes.

"Percy! Percy! Oh, Percy," shrieked the woman, clawing at her neck and hair.

Edwin put the baby on the ground and dashed to his car. Tearing open the rear door he grabbed the Indian blanket off the seat, unfolding it as he ran back. Wrapping it around her, he skillfully threw her over on the ground, still holding her with his strong arms, and rolled her over several times. He pulled the blanket open at her face. He did not want to smother her.

"Oh, my God," moaned Edwin, for at the same moment he looked at the woman's horribly burned face, he noticed angry flames shooting out two windows.

"Is someone else in the house?" he asked half choking. The woman on the ground answered with a painful moan. Was she dying? Her eyes were swollen half shut, and her lips were parched and ready to bleed.

Two men in a stock truck turned in. They saw at a glance help was needed and quick action was necessary. The older of the two began asking Edwin questions and told the younger to stand on the highway and hail the next car or run to the nearest telephone.

It was not long until the farmyard and the highway were lined with cars, and at least fifty persons were at the scene, shaking, stupidly helpless and horrified.

"Take care of the baby," demanded Edwin huskily, pointing to the bundle near the lilac bush. In his desperation at that moment he hardly realized to whom he was speaking. He did not care.

Someone, anybody must help. Seconds seemed hours. He forgot himself, his trip, his appointment at the dormitory. He even forgot the watch in his pocket. He was ready to run at any risk to save this poor woman and her little one.

Though the woman was a perfect stranger to him, he felt a moral obligation, a "must" for Christ's sake toward her. The desperate, pitiful look on her face gripped him. Edwin had young, red, heroic blood in his veins, and this woman was young, too, perhaps no older than himself. He told the other men to look after the house. He stayed by the stricken mother on the ground. Slowly, tenderly, he unwound the blanket, turning her over as carefully as possible. He spoke to her, called her "Mrs.," "lady," "friend," but only got groans for an answer.

Then that loud, piercing, shrieking sound of the fire engine's siren came. Someone had found a telephone. People moved back from the driveway. More motorists stopped, more people crowded around. Another higher-pitched siren was heard, and the ambulance arrived.

Edwin was kneeling on the grass beside the woman. If her time had come to die, was she ready? Did she know the Lord? He wanted to ask her. He wanted to know. This poor woman had suddenly come into his world. A mob of people gathered close trying to get a glimpse. They wanted to see, would see, must see, then shuddered after they had seen. Two young fellows rudely crowded their way between several women, almost knocking one over in an effort to see what the attraction was.

The larger of the two and the coarser-voiced got down on both knees behind Edwin, put both hands on Edwin's hips and hollered roughly into his right ear. "Purty nigh barbecued, ain't she?" he half chuckled, half sneered. Edwin shivered. It sounded so impossible, so brutal, so ignorant for anyone to make such a remark now. How could any human speak so boisterously, uncultured, and ill-mannered at such a time, even though the woman was a stranger?

Edwin drew his face away. He detected liquor on the man's breath. It nauseated him.

"Have a heart," Edwin reprimanded; "she might be dying. This is no time to talk lightly."

"Oh, well," blurted the other, "There's too many in this silly world anyhow." He pressed maddeningly close to Edwin again, and pressed both hands against his hips. The he scuffled awkwardly to his feet and was soon lost in the crowd.

The house was hopelessly ruined in spite of the efforts of the fire fighters. Mother and baby were rushed to the nearest hospital.

The crowd dribbled away one by one. There was nothing more to do but stand around and regret that such misfortunes happen, and hope such a catastrophe never could happen to anyone else.

Edwin looked at his watch. What! It's ten o'clock and I have two hundred miles yet to go? A startled, sickening feeling took hold of him. He could hardly realize how the time had slipped by. He hurried, half running to his car, and quickly as possible got on to the highway again. Traffic was heavy. He could not make much headway until he got out of the jam.

A strange combination of thoughts possessed him. One minute he knew he had done the only right thing—the only Christ-like thing. To have gone on would have been next to unforgivable. Laura Lou would have been heartily disappointed had he done that. He was certain of it. He had tried to be a friend in need, a comforter, a good Samaritan. But what would she think if at one o'clock, he was not there? Two o'clock? He could not make it before two now and drive with any degree of safety.

He would miss her solo. Edwin was sure of it, and he cleared his throat to swallow the lump of disappointment that kept coming up and up. He wasn't going to swallow the lump of disappointment that kept coming up and up. He wasn't going allow himself to feel uneasy or apprehensive over this. He'd stop in the next town and call her and explain it all. She'd understand. He had for years made Romans 8:28 his daily motto. Even as he drove along, he said it aloud. Not once, but several times. "And we know that all things work together for good to those that love the Lord."—and I do! "And I know that I love you God! I never loved you more than I do right now! To them that are called. I never was more sure of this before!"

Before Edwin finished his sentence to himself, the car began to sputter, then almost stopped. He stepped a little harder on the gas and pulled the choke. The car gave a jerk, went a few rods and sputtered again.

Then he remembered he had gone at least forty miles beyond the town where he intended to get gas. Edwin's strong arms sagged on the steering wheel. Scolding himself inwardly, he pulled off the highway and parked his car. He could go no farther. He drew out his hanky and wiped his damp forehead.

This now was his own fault. He had been thoughtless and forgetful. In his desperate concern for the dying mother, he had overlooked this all important thing. "According to His purpose," he repeated." Oh, dear God, your word is very true, so very true! But—

He flagged down the first car with his hat. It went by. It never even slowed down. He flagged the second. A little thin old man, so thin he was almost transparent, driving an old dilapidated jitney, stopped and called out in a squeaky but friendly voice. "Jump in, my friend. Spec' you're out of go-juice!"

"That's exactly it," answered Edwin, laughing with more merriment than he really felt. "I stopped along the way, back near Marousburg where there was a bad fire; then after I got on the road again, I guess I sorta forgot myself for a while."

"Yeh?" The thin man tilted his hat and scratched his bald head. "Well, I'll take you on into Bethby. That's the closest. I was agoin' a turn off a mile an' a quarter this side of Bethby, but I'll just tote you on in. Spec' I got the time."

"I'll pay you," Edwin said.

"Ho, ho!" laughed the little man good naturedly. "If I can't do that fer a feller without pay, I'd better git off the road. Maybe tomorrow, I might run out myself! Never can tell. Bad fire, was it?"

"Awful!" answered Edwin. "A young mother badly burned. I'm afraid she will die, if she hasn't already, and her small baby. . . . I don't know how I happened to be the first one to come along. It was about around nine o'clock I guess.

"Yes?"

"I wanted to be at Hempton Falls by one o'clock."

"Yes, won't make it, will you?"

"Never. My friend is being graduated. The chorus program is this afternoon. I will miss most of it now."

"Yeh? Spec' you will."

"I guess it's all for some purpose, although I can't see it now."

"Yeh. Well, that's the easiest way ter look at it, I 'spect."

"I'm terribly, terribly disappointed," and there was a lamentable note in Edwin's voice, "but I still believe Romans 8:28."

The man at the wheel squinted his small beadlike eyes and squirmed as though he were trying to work himself out of a knot.

"Guess that's Bible talk, ain't it?"

"That's right," replied Edwin. "I can't see why I'm not to make it to Hempton Falls by one, but I won't give up on believing that everything, even this stupid thing of running out of gas, will somehow work together for good, because I love God, and I've been called according to His purpose."

A long, almost awkward, pause followed, and Edwin expected the little man to say, "yeh" once more, but he didn't. Instead, he sniffled twice, then finally punctured the silence. "'Peers ter me that's 'bout as good a way o' looking at a thing as any." Then he chuckled and pointed in the distance.

"There's Hap's fillin' station ter the right. Want you to tote you back?"

The man scratched his bald head again, tilting his hat half off. He put it in place, squinted his black beady eyes, and sniffed twice.

"Spec' you will, if you keep on believin' your Bible ways."

"I intend to do that, sir. I thank you for this lift, and the good Lord bless you for your kindness. He does, doesn't he?"

"Yeh. Spec' He does, sorta."

"Are you a Christian, sir?"

Edwin was out of the jitney now. He would very likely never see this man again. Somehow, his genial, friendly manner impressed Edwin. With so thin and frail a body, how could he exist long? This little old man had suddenly, unexpectedly come into his world. He could not let him pass on without dropping a word about the thing that matters most in life.

For days, Edwin had prayed that his boss would grant him leave these two days, so he could go to Hempton Falls to bring Laura Lou home. With that request, he had promised God that he'd never let and opportunity go by to speak to persons he met about spiritual matters. If the love of Jesus Christ was a vital, living something within himself, and he knew it was, it was worth sharing, scattering, broadcasting. His own personal joy and satisfaction was in such abundance he could not contain it all.

"Sorta, sorta." The jitney driver was anxious to be on his way. He didn't enjoy squirming out of such knots too often, and yet he rather liked this chap who was responsible for getting him into it.

"I may never meet you again on this earth, my good friend," ventured Edwin with a serious but kind tone in his voice. "I know I'm in the Gospel bus that takes believers to heaven, and I want you to be sure you are in it too."

"Thank you, thank you fer your wish, young man. So long."

"So long friend, God bless you."

Edwin caught a ride to the filling station in a short time.

"I ran out of gas down the road several miles," he addressed the man who got up from his bench in front of his station to wait on him. "Can you fix me up a can to take back?"

"Guess we can if you pay for the can till you bring it back. I have to do it that way since several guys have gone off and never returned their cans. Two gallons enough?"

"Yes sir."

"That will be one-fifty, please."

"Yes sir."

"All right."

Edwin unbuttoned his hip pocket and reached for his billfold.

"No!

His pocket was empty. His billfold was gone!

Chapter 3

His billfold was gone! A frantic, almost distracting impulse struck him like a huge blow! It could have been no other but that rude fellow who had the smell of liquor on his breath, and had pushed himself so maddeningly through the crowd that knelt behind him. Why hadn't he expected such a thing? For a second, Edwin wanted to run back and try to catch that thief and turn him over to the police. He desperately needed his billfold! God knew he needed it. What am I going to do now? How can all this work together for the good for me? What can I do? Out of gas! Out of money! No driver's card! Not even a quarter in my pocket!

He was getting frantic. It took Edwin a long time to chase the anger and frustration away. His heart was breaking. Wasn't it God's will that he go see Laura Lou? What am I to do? It is unbelievable! Then an idea gave him a ray of hope. Maybe he could pawn the new watch! He took it out of his vest pocket and looked at it for a time. The man at the gas station guessed his predicament. He had watched the panic in his eyes.

"Would you?" asked Edwin, holding the watch in his hands.

"How do I know it's not stolen?" he asked

"You have nothing but my word," answered Edwin in a shocked, hurt voice.

"Well, I am at the place where I do not trust or take anyone's word from nobody no more."

Was it Edwin's lot to have nothing but misfortune and disappointment today? It seemed like an evil game in which fate was to be determined. What had he done to deserve such horrible reverses? His entire earnings of the past three months were in that stolen billfold. He had planned to stop at a good restaurant with Laura Lou on the way home. He had planned to treat her to the best. Only a few minutes before, he had testified to the jitney driver that he was going to believe—no matter what happened. Depressed, he walked slowly to a lawn chair beside the filling station and sat down to study.

"You don't mind if I sit here a while do you, sir?"

"I never allow loafers, but I guess you can rest a bit."

Edwin put his face in his hands. "Dear God in heaven," he prayed silently, "in Jesus' name, help me to know what to do. I don't want to sin now by doubting Thy word. If it's not good for now, it's not what I claimed it to be. You know, dear Lord, that Romans 8:28 has been my motto and it's got to still be! I do believe it. I dare not doubt, even though the devil wants me to. God bless that mean fellow who stole my billfold. I am one—one of Thy called ones according to Thy mysterious purpose, so deal with me, dear Father in Heaven, according to Thy will!"

Edwin Ferdella rose, stretched himself, and started walking briskly down the road running south. As he neared the first farm, he rolled up his dirty shirt sleeves that were spotted with holes. He knew he smelled of smoke and felt unpresentable. He opened his shirt collar.

The house he came to was a handsome two-story brick structure, and on either side of the driveway were rows of pine trees. The midday sun was hot and blindingly bright. He was not only very warm, but extremely thirsty. In his anxiety to get to his destination he had almost forgotten about eating. The savory odor of boiling ham met his nostrils.

With mixed feelings, he opened the iron yard gate and latched it behind him, and started up the cement steps at the back door. He waited.

Surely someone was at home, for the door stood wide open, and the meat was cooking on the open range. More than that, he was certain he had seen a figure in pink dart out of sight just as he raised his hand to knock.

He repeated the action—this time with a little more force. Again, he stood waiting. He could feel his heart pounding violently. It seemed to fill his chest.

A young girl, perhaps seventeen, came from the direction into which he had seen her dart. She was wearing a pink percale house dress. Slowly and almost reluctantly she moved toward the door. She had evidently just recently shampooed her hair, for it was hanging in damp strands around her shoulders, and her right hand held a comb.

"I beg your pardon," began Edwin, hat in hand. "But is the man of the house around?"

"No sir," came her precise answer. She never did come quite to the door. Perhaps she was afraid of him. Edwin tired to look pleasant and harmless.

"Is your mother here?"

"No sir." This she said with more exactness. She seemed to be even irritated.

"I'm looking for a job," he said.

"A job?" she scowled. She slapped the comb in the palm of her hand.

"I need work badly," Edwin began to explain. "I've had a misfortune on the road this morning. I stopped to give assistance where there was a fire back along the highway about fifty miles from here. I was robbed, and now I'm out of gas. My car is parked about four miles from here. I'd like to work enough to pay for a phone call and to buy a little gas. I have only fifteen cents on me.

"Oh, I," the girl behind the screen door kept shaking her head.

"I'm in an awful predicament. Couldn't I mow the lawn, or pull some weeds, or wash your car, or do something to earn a little? I have a very important phone call to make.

Through the screen door, Edwin could see the rigorous, strait-laced expression on the girls face. He could only read her thoughts. It seemed she doubted every word he spoke, and she'd be happy if he'd leave immediately. By all appearances she was alone in the house. On a chair beside the kitchen sink, was a picnic basket heaped full. On the table were three loaves of homemade bread, glossy on top from recent greasing.

"We have nothing for you to do." She announced sharply. "Nothing at all."

"Well, thank you for your bother," he said courteously, "but would you mind giving me a drink? I'm very thirsty."

The girl drew back as though perplexed or afraid. She made no effort to get him a drink.

"Very well," Edwin said. "I'm sorry I bothered you. If you don't mind, I'll stop out here by the edge of the garden and get a drink from the pump."

"It may not be working," she suggested.

Edwin Ferdella started down the steps. He almost felt hard toward the snobbish girl. Why had she treated him so high-handed and impolite? She could have at least given a stranger a glass of cold water on so hot a day. She had been hard and snappy without a reason. Unless, of course, she was frightened. Maybe she had been warned about strangers.

Puzzled over his plight, he stood for a moment by the rusty pump. The tin cup hanging on the pump was rusty also. The water was strange and tasted like old wet leaves. He drank two cups full. Less than two feet away from the pump, he noticed several luscious, almost-ripe strawberries. One or two might kill the unpleasant water taste in his mouth. He tuned to go. That, of course, would be stealing.

At the end of the lane Edwin noticed something small and shiny, half buried in the dust. He kicked it with the toe of his shoe. It was a key. He stopped and picked it up and slipped it into his pocket.

Inside the house Edwin had just left, the young girl's brother came bounding down the stairs, buttoning his shirt sleeves as he came.

"Bess," he exclaimed, "aren't you ready? Look at the clock. Isn't your hair dry yet?"

"Well, I have been hurrying as fast as possible, Arthur."

"I thought I heard you talking to someone a bit ago." Is Kenny here already?"

"No, it was a tramp."

"A tramp? What did he want?"

"Oh, something to do. A job. Said he was out of gas and had a fantastic made-up story. I didn't take the time to talk to him. Anyway, I think he was a fake. I didn't give him anything to eat either. I let him get a drink out at the pump."

"The pump? Out there? Why, Bessie Gordon, you—!"

"Well?"

"Why, Bessie, you knew there was a dead rabbit in that well. It's not good for anyone to drink. Not even a tramp."

"I don't care. I'm not going to hand water to a man I'm afraid of. If you had been down here, you would have thought he was scary too!"

"Well, get your hair up, Bess. Kenny will be here any minute now. The rest of the bunch will be waiting on us. The lunch is all packed?"

"Yes."

"I hope the man doesn't get typhoid fever or something like that!"

"Oh, he won't," answered Bess, a little aggravated. "If he was lying he must have typhoid!"

"You didn't hear what Brother White said in his sermon Sunday evening?"

"What?" Bess was walking away. She must hurry.

"About entertaining angels unawares sometimes."

Bess laughed mockingly. "I'm sure he wasn't an angel," she answered over her shoulder.

Chapter 4

Edwin trudged on to the next farmhouse. He walked an eighth of a mile. A middle aged woman met him at the front door. He hardly knew where to begin this time. He realized looked very untidy and that his story would sound absurd, even maybe fictitious, but there was no time to give up.

"Oh," he breathed, "if Laura Lou knew about what actually happened, she would fall to her knees."

Edwin answered the woman's "how do you do?" with a smile and began his story in a straight-forward manner.

"Hello, my name is Edwin Ferdella and I live in Haydren. I'm on my way to Hampton Falls where I had planned to find the graduation exercises at the College."

"But you are not on the right road for Hampton Falls," she interrupted.

"I know I am off a little. My car is parked along the highway about four miles west of here. I ran out of gas, and I wonder if you have a telephone I could use?"

"A telephone? Yes, come in." She opened the screen door. "It's right here by the dining room window, please help yourself."

"Thank you."

"Long distance, please. Give me Ferdella's residence at in Haydren, and reverse the charges."

Turning to the woman he asked, "What is this number?"

"5270W1."

"This is 5270W1. That's right."

It was not long until Edwin heard his father's voice.

"Father? This is Edwin. Don't be worried, but I need a little help. What? No. I'm not hurt. No, it wasn't an accident. No, but about nine o'clock I passed a house that was on fire, and a young mother was just coming out, and she had a baby in her arms. Oh, yes, I stopped of course. That's it. I had to help. It was pitiful. I was there an hour or more, and while I was in the crowd, someone stole my billfold. Yes, it's gone. Well, I had at least ninety in it. Yes, my driver's license, Laura Lou's picture, and all that. That's what I am calling home to tell you. I am stranded here near Bethby more than a hundred miles from Hempton Falls. I am out of gas too. I know it. Laura Lou won't know what to think. Oh, it's eleven-thirty here. Will you call Laura Lou for me and tell her what's happened? What? Well, I haven't enough money to put in a call, and I'd rather not reverse the charges. Oh, Father, that would be swell of you, if you'd to that, but unless I find a job, how can I get there? I tried to pawn her new watch that I was going to give her, at the filling station down the road, but the man talked as if he thought I had stolen it. No, no, he wouldn't take my word. Well, I'm here at a farmhouse using their phone. I couldn't make it by one o'clock even if I left now and actually had gas. Yes, I know, it's a terrible disappointment, and I don't know why it all had to go like this, but I guess it's for some purpose. Maybe, someday I will understand the purpose of it all. Yes. Then you'll call Laura Lou for me? Well, maybe that would be best too. If you called her before she sings, maybe she'd feel so bad she couldn't do her best. I know. Just a minute, Father, hold the line a minute."

The friendly faced woman had gone to the kitchen to turn her potatoes, but she heard everything, every word of Edwin's conversation. She came into the dining room and stood by him, tapping his arm lightly to get his attention.

"I'll help you out," she said consolingly. "I'll advance you some money on the watch so you can get there."

"Oh, would you? Would you really?" Edwin's face lit up with a glad smile.

"Father, I was talking to the lady of the house here and she said she'd give me some money on the watch—so I can go on. Yes. Then don't try to call her. I'll get there by the time the program is over. Yes. Yes. Good-bye, Father, and thanks a million."

"My father will telegraph me money," Edwin explained. He wanted to shout and dance and clap his hands. "He will send it to the college," he added, his face glowing radiantly.

He pulled the dainty watch case out of his vest pocket and handed it to the woman. She took it rather reluctantly and opened it carefully.

"Isn't it pretty?" she exclaimed. "I have an idea it's an engagement pres-ent, am I right?"

"No, not exactly. We've been engaged since Christmas, and I gave my fiancée a cedar chest then. This is a graduation present."

"It's a shame we have to do it this way, now isn't it?" She spoke sym-pathetically and with feeling. Edwin felt her understanding eyes search his warm face.

"Yes, it's sorta like a shame," he admitted, "but she'll understand. We'll stop here on our way back tomorrow and give it to her then."

"Oh, then I will get to meet her. How much do you want?" She started in the direction of the bedroom.

"Five might get me there."

"I'll give you ten. You'll be back with the money tomorrow?"

"Unless something as strange and unforeseen as all this happens. I'll be back tomorrow." She returned with a ten-dollar bill in her hand.

"And your name is?"

"I'll write it down for you."

"And mine is Mrs. Badger, Mrs. Jerome Badger. Here comes Mr. Badger now. Just wait, I'll ask him if he won't take you back to your car."

"Oh, that's expecting too much, Mrs. Badger," but Edwin's voice be-trayed the fact that he'd be obliged for the lift.

"Not at all." I know he will do it for you. Then I'd feel better about it too. You'll get there sooner—I mean a little sooner."

"Oh, Jerome dear," she called cheerfully. "Come in here and meet Mr. Ferdella from Haydern. He ran out of gas, Jerome, and I told him you'd take him back to his car. Take a little gas along dear, so he can get on the road sooner. You see, his friend is graduating from Hempton Falls College and he wants to be there by one."

"Sure enough," came Mr. Badger's ready response. "Come on out and get in. But you'll never make it by two now, unless you drive like Jehu."

"But your dinner, Mr. Badger," considered Edwin.

"Well, it has waited before, and I guess once more won't make any difference. The cook said I should."

"And how about your dinner, Mr. Ferdella?" Mrs. Badger inquired.

"I have my dinner in the car. Mother fixed it for me."

* * *

Davera Maloney slammed the front door and flopped herself down on the blue hassock. She kicked off both shoes, and tossed her chewing gum into the wastepaper basket.

"What's wrong now, honey?" asked her plump mother for the sixth time that week.

"You must not be feeling well. Everything seems to upset you. What now, Davera?"

"Everything." Davera took off her rose tinted glasses and rubbed her eyes.

"Everything?"

"Well, just about," she sighed.

"Something new?"

"I guess it's not new exactly," she pouted. "But I just heard this evening that Edwin Ferdella went off without me!"

"Off where?"

"Why, to Hempton Falls, of course. He knew very well I wanted to go along out and see Joan."

"He did?" questioned her mother's subdued voice. She must handle Davera delicately.

"Of course, he did. He heard me say so often enough. I know he did. He might have known anyway, as well as he knows I like Joan. What's more, Dad would have been willing to pay him well—even let him make money on the trip."

"But, Davera honey," pleaded her mother, "you mustn't act like this. I suppose Edwin wanted to select his own passengers."

"That's just it!" she shouted irritably.

"He's so very selective! He thinks that he can just look at another girl, that stuck-up Laura Lou Gentry."

"Davera dear," whispered her mother.

"Well, I mean just that. She thinks she is so smart and she's more common than I am. Here, her dad gave Edwin a chance to make good in the store, and he was too blind and stupid to see it. Couldn't see money when it was stuck right under his nose, and then he took a job at the dairy. I don't care!

"Then don't feel so bad about it, Davera." Just don't care. Try not to."

"But you know I do care. You know that, Mother! They'll never be happy if they marry." Davera was nearly out of breath now.

"Laura Lou's gone off and got herself a college education so she can teach. But I'll bet she can't work as hard as I can or do as many things as I can. She can't skate, she can't play tennis worth watching, she can't swim, she can't play anything but prattle on the piano. She—"

"She can sing," ventured Mother.

"Oh, and how!" hooted Davera. I never could see anything so marvelous about her weakly voice. It lacks color and everything, just like she does. She's drab and common and just down ordinary. It makes me plain mad to think that she's getting Edwin Ferdella. How she did it, I can't understand! It's beyond me. He's got no sense of beauty, any values of taste or anything."

"Well, honey," mumbled Mrs. Maloney feebly, "everyone don't see alike."

"They most certainly don't" agreed Davera. "And I never will be able to understand that Edwin. He never did give me a real chance to show myself. I'm smart and talented. I'm talented much more than her!"

"Go upstairs and take a shower. You're tired. Rest a while and forget Edwin. Then come down and gather a fresh bouquet for the table."

"It's easy to say to forget, but it's not so easy to do it!"

"I know dear, but— but—" Mrs. Maloney hesitated. Should she say it? Dare she say it? She coughed nervously, wiped her forehead, then ventured timidly. Davera always had been a nervous, peevish child. "Her Aunt Susetta passed me on the avenue that afternoon and said they were getting married in September.

"In September!"

"Shush. Not so loud, Davera. Someone is walking by."

"It's about the stupidest outfit I have ever heard of along while Laura Lou's not even what I would call pretty."

"Run along dear. Take your bath."

"I will! I'll take a good long beauty bath. I'll show Edwin he's not the only pebble on this beach!"

Chapter 5

The director stepped to the right and stood almost motionless, directing the chorus with the slightest movements of his fingers. The interest of the audience now was on one person, the modest, sweet-faced girl in the foreground. With serious reverence and intelligent appreciation for sacred music, she had studied and set herself the task of learning her assignment well. With all the feminine volume required, Laura Lou sang, now tenderly, now vigorously, shifting from one emotion to another with splendid and extraordinary beauty. Those few who had been fanning laid their fans in their laps.

Some even bent forward.

Oh, holy night, thou art descending,
Bringing with thee sweetest dreaming,
Like the moonlight's silvery beaming,
Flooding every aching breast.

The chorus hummed.

And the soul finds soothing rest;
Calling to thy early light.
Come again, oh, Holy Night.
Bring us dreams that have no ending.
Dreams of Christ, our blessed Savior.
Christ and God, the Lord and Father.

Without trying Laura sang with warm dramatic power. It expressed her inner religious conviction that spelled devotion and energy and talent. Every music lover in the audience felt a personal invitation to share in the beauty of her song and in the joy of God's full grace in Jesus Christ, which she sang about and which was reflected on her young wholesome face.

"Look down, holy dove, Spirit now. . . ."

Her deep blue eyes glowed with a heavenly light as she continued her song. The harmony was true and beautiful, and the final chord strong and true.

Laura Lou took her seat, conscious of the fact that the Lord had helped her do her best. Although she had failed to find Edwin's face in the crowd, something inspired her with earnest hope to present her contribution as though he were there. Thoughtfully, she anticipated meeting him at the close of the program. He would search her out. She would meet his eyes. He had said he was coming. He would be there.

Almost unconsciously she prayed, for turning to God for every desire and problem had become so much a part of her, she could do it anytime and anywhere without thinking. She prayed that whenever he was at the moment, the guardian angel of the Lord would be attending him and that, although she was disappointed in not having met him before the program as planned, they would be together before another hour passed.

Quietly Edwin swung into the first parking space he could find. He looked at his watch. Even with a short stop to wash and change clothes and eat part of his lunch, he believed he had arrived before the chorus program was concluded. He looked toward the auditorium. People were just beginning to come out; he watched the walks become a swarming, moving mass. Some people were shaking hands, loitering to talk to old friends, while others were going directly to their cars, and still others were hurrying to the dormitories for luggage, bags, and boxes. The spirit of summer vacation was in the air. He headed toward the side door where he saw the chorus members leaving the auditorium.

Before she saw him, she felt his warm hand on her arm. Two ladies in front of him obstructed her view. He had to reach past them to stop her or she would have gone by.

"Laura Lou," he called out affectionately.

"Oh, Edwin! Oh, you did get here, didn't you?" Their glad eyes met.

The two women chuckled, stepped aside, and said in a low voice, "Guess we're taking up too much room, Sara. What shall we do with ourselves, anyway? At every place we try to stand, we're in somebody's way. I have never seen such a crowd at Hempton Falls in thirty years."

Edwin drew Laura Lou closer to himself.

"I just now came."

"Then, then you weren't here for the program?"

"No, dear. I missed it, but God knows how hard I tried go get here on time."

"I looked and looked. Once I thought sure it was you who came in the side door, then I saw it wasn't you after all. When you did not call for me at the dormitory, I thought that perhaps you came late and went on in. Then I looked from the front seat to the back and up into the balcony, but I could not find you. So I prayed."

"Yes?"

"Yes, Edwin, I had to keep down the fear that something might have happened to you."

"Something did happen, Laura Lou."

"Very bad, Edwin? Oh, surely, not a wreck?" She caught her breath and held it.

"No dear, not that."

"You look perfectly all right, Edwin."

"I am. And how perfectly beautiful you are in this lovely dress." His kind eyes scanned her tenderly, admiringly. "It is very becoming to you!"

"Thank you Edwin—but you must tell me what happened. Don't keep me wondering any longer."

He took her hand. "Shall we find a place first where we can be alone? The whole town seems to be here today, and every graduate must have a host of relatives."

"Let me see," she pondered. "Where could we go?" The reception rooms are full."

"Then, let's go over to my car. I had to park it down the avenue."

Before they reached the fountain, the call came over the loud speaker.

"Attention please," came a strong, clear voice again. "A telegram for Edwin Ferdella, in care of Laura Lou Gentry. Call for it at the president's office."

Edwin saw the look of alarm on Laura Lou's face.

"Don't be alarmed, dear, I know what it is. Go with me and show me where the president's office is."

Now every person on the campus knew the name Edwin Ferdella,was linked with that of Laura Lou Gentry's, the pretty girl who had sung the soprano solo. Conversations suddenly turned to a new topic. "Is that him? There they go."

At the door they met Mamie face to face. Laura Lou introduced Edwin. Mamie smiled pleasantly and said, "Well, he did get here, didn't he, Lulie? We knew he would. Your solo was beautiful, Laura Lou."

Edwin was on his way to the president's office. He really didn't have time to stop and talk to Mamie or anyone else. He wanted to get to the car and explain everything to Laura Lou.

"He didn't get here in time to hear it, Mamie."

"I'm sorry." Mamie touched her room-mate's hand affectionately.

"Mr. Ferdella," a tall broad-shouldered man came down the steps to meet him, holding out his hand. He caught Edwin's and shook it warmly, smiling at Laura Lou.

"I am delighted to meet you," he smiled. "I am Collin Echerborn, a member of the school board where Miss Gentry is going to be teaching."

"I am glad to meet you, Mr. Echerborn." Edwin shook the older man's hand. "Very glad to meet you too."

"Did you get your telegram?"

"Not yet. I'm on the way to the president's office now."

"Then don't let me detain you—but I am very glad I heard the announcement, otherwise I wouldn't have known you were here. Go get your telegram, and then I'd like to talk with you just a little bit, if I may. I sincerely hope it's nothing serious, Mr. Ferdella."

"No, Mr. Echerborn, I know it is nothing serious, I was expecting it. I can talk with you right now, I think."

"You better go get your telegram first or they'll be sending the call out again thinking you didn't hear it."

"You are right. That's what I will do."

Together Edwin and Laura Lou entered the president's office. President Lindicott himself was there and handed the telegram to Edwin. Edwin nodded and smiled.

"Thank you, President Lindicott."

"You're welcome, Mr. Ferdella. Let me shake your hand and congratulate you on being fortunate in winning so lovely a lady." He motioned to Laura Lou. His serious gray eyes twinkled with respect and sincerity.

"Thank you, thank you, President Lindicott. I am fortunate but it's more than just luck or favor. I can't help but feel God has had a definite hand in this, otherwise I doubt if I could ever have won her. God really brought us together."

Edwin stuck the telegram into his inside jacket pocket without opening it.

"How very much I wish more of our young people felt that way," spoke the president. "We have endeavored to give special spiritual guidance emphasis to romance at this school, particularly during the past school year, and yet I have seen again and again that some students have failed to catch the significance of letting God lead. It is very important. It means lifelong happiness and service to the church, or lifelong misery and regrets. God bless both of you. I understand, Laura Lou, that you will be teaching in the new Christian day school at Penderson."

"That's right. I am thrilled about it, but I want you to remember me in your prayers. It will be a new experience for me, and I do not want to be a disappointment to the church or my college or the school board."

"You can depend upon our prayers, Laura Lou. Nothing gives me more satisfaction and genuine happiness, than knowing our graduates go out from this school to serve our church. Far too many go into business which only exalt themselves or give them a time in the world. It is then that I feel our schools have failed. It grieves me beyond my words to express it." His one hand went firmly down on top of his desk, and with the other he removed his horn-rimmed glasses. "We must somehow give our students a vision of the need of staying by the church in service. There is an ever-increasing demand for conscientious, consecrated workers, and yet with all our cultured, top-notch students, not enough are willing to answer these calls. Sometimes I think my heart will break, when I read over the alumni notes and see the names of men and women who thought were here preparing for Christian Service today, out in the world, heaping upon themselves money by the tens of thousands, while the church is suffering and the schools have to beg for money, the mission boards scour the country for workers and funds to carry on. Truly, we are living the midnight hour of this age."

Tears crept into the president's intelligent, thoughtful eyes. He blinked them away. Smiling seriously, he gripped Edwin's arm. "Go out to serve the church, my friend," he said in a low voice, "and God bless your efforts. You've never been here as a student, except for a winter Bible term, a time or two, if I recall correctly, but Laura Lou has been one of our faithful, loyal students, and I am sure that whatever worthwhile work you undertake, she will be a real supporter in it."

"She will—that I know," and Edwin smiled down on Laura Lou with joyed enthusiasm.

As they left the president's office, Miss Manche waited for them. "Laura Lou," came her musical voice. "I heard the music over the loud speaker and rushed back to hear and see you. I wanted to meet your friend." She held out her hand.

"Oh, yes, Miss Manche. Edwin, this is my teacher, Miss Manche. My fiancé Edwin Ferdella.

"How do you do? I came back to ask you to our home for supper at six o-clock. You won't be leaving tonight yet, will you?"

"No, we planned to leave in the morning." Answered Laura Lou. "Isn't that right, Edwin?"

"Yes, that is what we planned."

"Oh good, then you'll come, won't you?

"My mother will be pleased. She has taken a special liking to Laura Lou." This she addressed to Edwin, "and nothing would please me more than to meet you, Mr. Ferdella. By the way, we have all kinds of room at our house, too. Everyone is leaving this afternoon. You might as well both stay with us tonight. The dormitory will be desolate. Laura Lou, will you come?"

Edwin looked at Laura Lou for the answer. "It would be lovely to stay with you, Miss Manche."

"I am glad!" laughed Miss Manche. "I'll run along now and have things ready until you get there."

"But please don't go to any bother," Laura Lou said thoughtfully. "Just a little something will be alright."

Miss Manche laughed.

"Mother will want you to sing for her."

"Sing?"

"Yes, dear. You must sing your solo for her. She was heartbroken she didn't get to come today. I know it won't be the same without the chorus, but sing it for her anyway. Mother may never get to hear you sing it again. Mr. Ferdella, my mother is eighty-one. She has taken a great fancy to Laura Lou. We will both miss her. Have you seen the picture she made of my little niece sitting by Mother's knee?"

"No, I haven't yet."

"You will love it. I know. I must say this yet before I go, and I say it with no impingement of conscience or flattery, that Laura Lou has been a delightful student. She is original and practical. I'm glad I hadn't gone on home before the announcement."

Laura Lou blushed a deep peach pink.

Chapter 6

Mr. Echerborne was waiting, hat in hand, in the hall as Edwin and Laura Lou waved good-bye to Mrs. Manche. He spoke in low tones. People were standing in the hall.

"I don't want to detain you two very long, but since I heard your names called over the loud-speaker, I knew at once now was my chance to speak to you together. You see a close friend of mine told me you've had experience working in a grocery store." He looked at Edwin. Their eyes met on the level.

"I've had experience, yes."

"Well, I own a store in Penderson, a nice super market with good trade. I'm looking for a young man who will take a live interest in the store. A Christian man, if you please, who can be trusted to take full oversight next winter while my wife and I go to California. We have been waiting to go out for the past seven years since her only sister moved to Los Angeles. So far, we've never been able to get away. You've been recommended to me, and since Miss Gentry will be teaching at Twin Hills, and since I heard you are getting married, I thought that perhaps you'd consider the job. If you'd consider it, I'll talk about wages, and I will treat you right."

Edwin's face glowed. How should he answer? What should he think? His mind jumped back to the very first thought of administration for Laura Lou Gentry. Why hadn't he decided yet on a job? Why had he been detained on this trip? Why a dozen other things?

"I will consider your proposition, Mr. Echerborn. I worked in a grocery store for several years, and I liked the work very much. I enjoyed meeting people. Recently I decided to change because," he hesitated. Why tell this stranger that the employee's daughter bored him, disgusted him, tried to tempt him? "I thought I'd like to work at the dairy for a change and I got a little more pay after six months."

"I see."

"I do have a conscience, however, against selling cigarettes or tobacco. I should tell you now."

"You don't need to, Mr. Ferdella. I handle neither. Lots of people told me I'd have to lock my doors unless I handled them, but I promised God if He'd bless my business He'd get His share of the profits, and it's surprising how He's blessed me. I am glad you feel as I do on this point. If you are interested, I'd like you to come out to look the place over. I'll talk business over my desk and show you some figures. There's a real chance for the right man. From September to December, you could tell whether or not you'd be interested in keeping on. You could start working in July or August for that matter. The sooner the better as far as I am concerned. And before it slips my mind, I have a little four-room house on the edge of town that will be empty in August. The people who are living in it now built a new house."

Laura Lou's eyes danced with happy excitement. She slipped her slender hand into Edwin's strong one, and pressed it gently. He drew a deep breath and smiled down at her.

"This may be rather sudden, I know. You don't need to give me your answer now. Another thing I might mention is this, we need a young man like you to help out in our Sunday School. Write me in a week or so. Laura Lou knows my address. Good-bye now."

"Edwin," whispered Laura Lou. He bent his ear toward her. "What does it all mean?"

"It means—well dear, dear girl, what could it mean, but that God is working together for us—for our good, because He loves us," he whispered.

"And because we love Him too." She added.

"Where can we go and get away from people?" he asked a little desperately. Yet he chuckled.

"Isn't it awful?" she laughed. "You haven't even had a chance to tell me what happened and why you were late, and about the telegram."

"Laura Lou, let us find the car before any else stops us."

"Do you suppose that will be possible, Edwin? Every person on campus knows now that you are here."

He pressed her hand. "And that I'm in care of Laura Lou Gentry." He laughed softly.

"Do you care?"

"Care?" I'm perfectly thrilled over that part of it. What other name would I rather be linked with? It'll be time to go to supper before we get to talk—unless we get started soon."

But before they were across the campus walk half a dozen people stopped to shake hands, to congratulate Laura Lou on her solo, and more than that—to meet her friend, Mr. Ferdella, whose name the had heard over the microphone. And at the iron gate at the entrance they met a couple with tennis rackets.

"Oh, Laura Lou," smiled the red-headed girl, "meet my cousin, Don Brackman. Is this your fiancé? I knew it. I heard the call." She laughed a bubbling laugh. "Say, we want you two to go along and play a game of tennis with us. Will you?"

"I'd love to Sally, but you see Edwin just arrived after the program and we haven't had a chance to talk yet. Pardon me, Sally. Edwin, I do want you to meet Sally Porter. Sally, Edwin Ferdella. And hello, Don."

"But, you're going to have all the way home to talk aren't you, Laura Lou?"

"Yes."

"Then come and play a game with us before you leave Hampton Falls."

"But, I'm in my good dress yet."

"You could change in a few minutes. Edwin, do you know how well she can play?"

"We haven't played in over an year now."

"Well, she's right there—just like she is with everything else she tries."

"I wouldn't doubt that, Sally. If Laura Lou wants to take time to play a game of tennis, I'll go along with her."

"I really better turn down your invitation this time, Sally, much as I know I'd enjoy it. We've been invited out for supper and I have a few other little things to look after before we go. Thanks Sally, but let me off this time."

"Now, tell me all about it Edwin." They were in his car at last.

"I will, Laura Lou, but first let us drive downtown to the Western Union office. This telegram will instruct the Western Union office to issue a bank draft in my name. Then I'll need to return to the business office at the college and get it cashed."

"Then we can drive out by the dam. There is a nice little park there and it is quiet except for the water."

"I believe with a firm heart," Edwin said as he began his story of the day's happening, "that God has brought us together and that God allowed all the experiences of this day for a purpose." He looked at the girl beside him with fond affection. "You know, I believe that if we commit our ways to God and trust Him, He will work out things for our personal good and bring things to pass that we never even dreamed of. I started out this morning at daybreak thinking I would meet you at the dormitory as we had planned. But circumstances changed my plans.

"You know, Laura Lou, I believe we each have a personal devil, who would ruin our lives, if he could. He would have me turned into a fatalist today, believing that God is unjust and cruel, but I can see now those fatalistic ideas he wanted me to have, would only have filled my heart with defeat and false destiny, But—"

"Why, Edwin, what do you mean?"

"Well, God knew I prayed for weeks I'd get to come today."

"Yes?"

"And God knew how happy I was when I started out this morning. I even sang as I was driving—I was so happy thinking about meeting you and being with you. God knows too, how I dreamed about listening to you sing your song.

"Yes Edwin, I was so disappointed when you didn't show up. For a moment or two I thought maybe I couldn't sing."

"You did?"

"But then I prayed. I asked God to please keep you from harm and bring you safety and help me to somehow get through the song without a blunder. And he did, didn't He?"

"And He brought me even though I was late, and I am sure you did very well—perfectly. I know."

"But hurry on. What next?"

"Well, about nine o' clock I passed a house that was on fire. Not only a house, but a mother and small baby. I stopped."

"Of course you did! You couldn't have gone on. I know your kind heart."

"I was the only one there for a while. I just happened to be going by. I know God planned it so I could help. I ran over and tore off my poplin jacket, and threw it around the woman to try to put the fire out. It was coming up her back and around her shoulders and to her hair. It was horrible!

"And the baby?"

"Pity, concern, and horror was written on the lady's face. I don't know if the lady and baby died or not. No one knows how the fire started and I have no idea, but I am afraid the woman died. It was horrible! I am afraid that she died. She was unconscious and they took her and the baby to the hospital. I don't even know the woman's name, but when we go home, I can show you where it happened."

"Then it was because of the fire that you were late?" Did the house burn down too?"

"Almost all ruined." I was there at least an hour, but while I was there trying to take care of the woman and the baby, some man came up behind me and stole my billfold out of my pocket. Then I ran out of gas and at that time discovered my billfold had been stolen.

"Oh Edwin, what did you do?"

"What could I do, but walk to a farmhouse and ask to call home. So I used their phone and called home and Father said he would wire me some money. I never got a look at the man who stole my money. I was so concerned about the baby and mother. Then I ran out of gas!"

"I still wonder how you got here if you were robbed and out of gas. How did you manage?"

"Well, dear, the Lord led me to a house where a kind-hearted woman let me use her telephone to call home, and she believed me enough to loan me ten dollars. On our way home we need to stop and repay her for her kindness. I told her I wanted to get here in time to see you graduate."

"I am glad I didn't know all of this or I would not have been able to sing."

"All the time I was coming to you as fast as I could, and you will never know how I needed your prayers little girl of mine. Tomorrow on the way home I will tell you more about what else happened to me. But right now, let's talk about what Mr. Echerhorn had to say. How did it sound to you?"

For a moment, Laura Lou sat thinking. The sun lay warm and shimmering on the quiet lawn. A gentle breeze blew folds of her white chorus dress around her slender ankles. Then she lifted her blue eyes to his, and her lips broke into a smile.

"I know that God has been working things out for your good, because if it hadn't been for the telegram and the call, Mr. Echerhorn would not have known you were here."

"But tell me, Laura Lou, what do you think about the offer he made?"

"It sounds all right and good to me and for you, because Mr. Echerborn wouldn't have known that you were here on the grounds if it wasn't for the telegram and the call."

"His offer is certainly worth considering, if you feel you'd like that sort of work. But you must decide."

"What time is it getting to be? Maybe we should be starting back. We don't want to make Miss Manche wait on us." Edwin looked at his watch. "If supper if served at six, then we need to be going."

"I'd like to go back to the dormitory and change my dress."

"OK then, my sweet girl. I know you are anxious to go home and we are both wondering how your Mother is. Have you seen her lately?"

"She was over last evening. She really looks much better. To be honest, six weeks ago I was somewhat alarmed about how she has been doing. Father is taking such good care of her and she is improving splendidly. I've appreciated watching over his tender attentions to her. Over and over I have resolved in my heart that I'm going to be that good to you."

"Come, dear, take my arm. Let's walk around for a little while. I want to tell you how wonderful and precious you are to me."

They walked towards the car, and all the way Edwin weighed his thoughts with his emotions. The prospects of the near future fed the flame of love in his heart. Could it be true, that Laura Lou felt happiness to that extent this sweet friend who had promised to be his wife? His soul went heavenward in a silent prayer of thankfulness. He knew that as long as he'd live, he'd never be able to forget the sweet picture of her loveliness as she walked beside him. Her face was radiant with it's sacred womanly charm. He felt new responsibility to live above the sin of the world and devote his entire life and soul to God and the church. She inspired him in an upward way. Since she had more education than he, then he knew he must be certain to spend more time in prayer. He must perform his duties in the church to the best of his ability. Their little chat had revealed to him again his sweetheart's striking Christian characteristics, and he felt a new challenge to a great adventure spiritually. It filled him with strength within his whole being.

Chapter 7

Laura Lou was trembling with joy as she waited for her call to go through. Her mother answered. "Hello, Mother. How are you? Good. I'm fine. We're about half way home. Yes, we're on our way home.

Everything's just lovely and fine. I just thought I'd like to call and tell you that if nothing happens, we'll be home by about 4 p.m. No. Oh it is? It's not raining here, but it's a bit cloudy in the west. Yes, Yes, Mother, Edwin gave me the prettiest watch. Yes, tell Daddy hello for me. We'll be seeing you after a while, and listen, Mother—please don't get excited because we are coming. Oh, she is? That's nice of her, isn't it? It's not raining here, but it is a little overcast. Tell Daddy hello for me. Oh, she is? That's nice of her. We'll see you after a while. Bye now."

"Your mother always wants things spic and span when she knows I'm coming home. Thanks, Mrs. Badger, for letting me use your telephone."

"You're entirely welcome, dear, and much happiness to both of you. It's been a real pleasure to meet you. I still feel guilty for keeping the watch."

"That's alright, Mrs. Badger. And after all," added Edwin, "I couldn't blame you. I was a perfect stranger. I had stopped first at the house down the road, but the young girl was there alone, and she seemed somewhat afraid of me."

He had driven past the driveway when he came to a sudden stop. He reached in his pocket and fumbled a little, then pulled out a small key.

"What is it Edwin?"

"I just happened to think of something. I stopped first at this place yesterday and asked for a job so I could get some money to buy a little gas."

"Where you said the girl acted so cool?"

"Yes, as I came away, I saw this key on the ground right back there at the end of the lane. Maybe I'd better go back and ask if it belongs to them."

"Let me see it Edwin. I don't know, of course," she turned it over on the palm of her hand. "But it wouldn't take but a minute to go in and find out. It's no good to us.

"Edwin backed his car past the driveway and turned in and met the same girl, this time in a yellow dress and plastic apron. He turned and met a man at the screen door. The family had evidently just finished the noon meal and was still standing around the kitchen table discussing something of interest. The young man beside the girl looked up. His mouth dropped open, he took two steps toward the door and raised both hands above his head.

"Edwin Ferdella!" he shouted. "Am I seeing things—or is it really you? Edwin! Borden, Arthur Borden!"

"I can hardly believe my eyes! Where did you come from? And where are you going?" Borden asked in one breath, throwing open the screen door. "And where have you been keeping yourself?"

Mr. and Mrs. Borden stood speechless, and in the background stared the girl in yellow, with a strange bewildered, almost frightening expression on her face. She was biting her lip nervously.

"Come on in, Edwin," motioned Arthur. "I want Mother and Father to meet you. Mother, this is Edwin Ferdella. Dad and Bess, come over here." Edwin shook hands with both Mr. and Mrs. Borden, but when it was the girl's turn, she stepped up shyly and rubbed her hand across the forehead.

"I am ashamed to let you shake my hand," she said feebly, and her cheeks got red in spots. Her brown eyes welled up with sudden tears.

"I—why I had no idea," she said with trembling lips.

"Forget it," said Edwin good-naturedly.

"I know I looked—"

"Oh! Arthur," she cried, "this—" She hid her crimson face in both her hands, "is the man I called a tramp yesterday." She wanted to run and hide.

"What! You mean? Why, Bessie Arlene Borden!"

"Well," she blinked through her tears, "you needn't make me feel worse that I do. I'm sorry. I didn't know."

"Cheer up Bessie," spoke Edwin gravely but with feeling. "You didn't hurt me. The lady down the road helped me out. You didn't know my name. How could you have guessed who I was?"

"Mrs. Badger?" she cried. "And she knows all this?"

"No not all, Bessie. Cheer up, please."

"Yes, but, I never—even—gave you a drink—and I let you get it your-self—at the pump. Oh, I feel so awful!"

"Now wait a minute here," began Mr. Borden with fatherly fervor in his voice, "let me talk a little. Arthur, is this the Edwin that . . ." he faltered. He tried to swallow the lump that came up in his throat.

"Yes Dad, this is the Edwin Ferdella who saved my life."

Mr. Borden grabbed Edwin's hand and clasped it firmly in both his brawny ones. Tears trickled down his full, wind-blown cheeks. "I've wanted to meet you for years. God bless you, my boy. I owe you my personal word of thanks."

Edwin was quite taken back. He stood for a moment in an almost unbelievable daze. Finally he collected himself. "I deserve no thanks, Mr. Borden," he said. "I did nothing more than my duty."

"Yes, you say that now, but Arthur has often told me you risked your own life to save him from drowning."

"Yes," nodded Edwin, meekly, "but I think Arthur would have done it for me or anyone else."

Bessie slipped into the bathroom to wet her hot face. How could she ever again meet this man whose name had often been mentioned with highest regard and reverence in their home during the past years? It scorched her. Could God forgive her? She had been lauding, admiring Edwin Ferdella, whom she had never seen, but who had saved her dear and only brother from drowning. It had been the most talked about happening of all Arthur's C.P.S. experiences.

"Your dinner," put in Mrs. Borden, tapping Edwin on the arm. "Let me fix—"

"No, indeed, Mrs. Borden," came Edwin's courteous answer. "Thank you, but we had our dinner in Lateen."

"And who's we?" Arthur looked toward the parked car.

"My fiancée is with me. I went over to Hempton Falls yesterday to get her. We're on our way home."

"Well, go get her. Bring her in. We've got to meet her, too."

"We haven't got long to stay, but I do want you to meet her. She's the best girl in all the world—the one meant just for me."

After Edwin brought Laura Lou into the house, half an hour slipped away before they realized it. Arthur and Edwin had many questions to ask about each other regarding what had transpired during the years since they had been together at camp.

"You see, Arthur," explained Edwin, "after we separated in Chicago that day, I spent six months helping my uncle in Dardix. Then I had a chance to go on a cattle boat to Poland. I enjoyed it very much. I spent a year in construction work in Belgium. I wrote you a letter once, and it came back unclaimed, so I concluded you were lost from me for the time being. But always, I kept hoping I'd run into you, or get in contact with you some way."

"And what brought you here today?"

"Oh, by the way, I almost forgot what I did stop for. It certainly wasn't because I knew you lived here, but," he held out the key which he had returned to his pocket in order to shake hands. "Yesterday I noticed this little key on the ground as I left the driveway. I stuck it in my pocket and almost passed your place today, before I thought about it. Is it yours by chance?"

Mr. Borden's eyes danced with excitement. He took the key and announced immediately, "It's the key to my strong box! You found it out on the road?"

"Yes sir."

"Well, I do declare! I have been looking high and low for three days!"

"You never told me you lost the key and was hunting for it!" broke in Mrs. Borden.

"No, Mary, I was afraid you'd worry if you knew it was lost, so I just kept looking for it, thinking it would turn up." He drew a long breath of relief and smiled with great appreciation. "But I never expected you'd turn up with it."

"Well, you know, Mr. Borden," Edwin said solemnly, "God for sure had a hand in this! If I hadn't run out of gas and I hadn't been robbed,

I wouldn't have stopped. I wouldn't have known that you live here. And, if I wouldn't have stopped, I wouldn't have noticed the key. The little key helped us, I mean the little key and the Lord helped us to find each other!"

"How true, how true!" answered Mr. Borden, with gratitude in his voice. "Wait just a minute please."

In a few minutes he returned and handed Edwin a sealed envelope.

"Here is a little gift for you."

"For me? Why, Mr. Borden?"

"Because I want to give it to you. I had something like this in mind for several years now. God has wonderfully blessed me and I am mighty thankful you came back with the key."

Wondering, Edwin took the envelope and began opening it.

"Don't open it now," suggested Mr. Borden pleasantly. "Wait until you are on your way. God bless you both! And drop in to see us whenever you are near this way."

"Thank you, Mr. Borden. And after we get settled in our home, I want you to come to see us. All of you come whenever you can. Tell your sister to come too. I may have looked like a tramp, but she will know me next time. Tell her not to feel bad about this."

Soon they were back on the road.

"Open it, Laura Lou, and see what it is!" Edwin suggested to Laura as he handed her the envelope.

"Oh! Edwin! Look. Just look, Edwin. Can you imagine this?"

"Money?"

"Why, Edwin, it's one hundred dollars!

"No!"

"It is! Here are five twenty dollar bills! Just think, that's more than was stolen from you!—and here's a slip which says, 'Gratitude to you for saving our son.'"

"I am not worthy of it! How can I take it?"

"But it would hurt them if you wouldn't accept it."

"I suppose so."

They passed the ruins of the little burned home. It was a gloomy picture of desolation and loss. The woman at the next farm where they stopped said that they buried the mother and baby the next afternoon. Laura took Edwin's hand. "I am so glad you did what you could for them."

"I just hope the mother passed safe in the arms of Jesus."

They rode on several miles in silence.

"Laura Lou," Edwin said, breaking the silence. "Look in the glove compartment and get out the Bible. I found a verse the other day and marked it. I want to make sure that I remember the words correctly. I am sure my Bible is in there."

When she opened the small metal door, a letter slipped out and fell to her feet. She picked it up.

"What is this?" she asked.

"I don't know, but it has your name on it." She held it up so she could see it more clearly.

"Go ahead and open it."

"Why, Edwin, you say you don't know anything about this? It's signed Davera. Why, Edwin!"

There was an tinge of disappointment in her voice. She gasped in astonishment. "You mean that Davera Maloney is still trying to get between us?"

"But she can't, darling!" He brought the car almost to a standstill. "I tell you the truth, Laura Lou, this is absolutely a surprise to me. Read it quickly. I can't figure out how it got in there!"

Laura Lou sat up very straight. Her breath came faster. "Dear Edwin," she read. "I would be very much delighted if you would take me along when you go to Hempton Falls."

"Well, of all the—"

"Go ahead dear!"

"A little bird told me you are going. You probably don't know it, but I have a very dear friend there I'd love to surprise. My father will gladly pay for the gas for the round trip. He says I need a vacation."

Laura Lou stopped abruptly, and a shifted cry escaped from her lips. "Why, Edwin Ferdella, what does this mean? Please explain it to me." Her voice was baffled and annoyed.

"The only explanation I can give, my dear, is that Davera Maloney is altogether mistaken if she imagines she can gain any headway with me, and she is absolutely out of her place to be sticking notes in my car."

"But has this happened before, Edwin? Has she been writing you letters?"

"NO! Never!"

"Never?"

"NEVER!"

There was a sudden sigh of relief.

"We've been so happy all day. Please don't let this spoil our happiness together. I have been true and faithful to you, Laura Lou. To the best of my knowledge, I have given her no reason at all to write such a note. I didn't even know that she knew I was coming out to pick you up."

"Then, why this note?"

"I do not know why. Your guess is as good as mine. I am sure she is jealous of you."

"You think?"

"What else could it mean, dear heart?"

"But she has no right to push herself in like this!"

"She has no right to, sweetheart, and she gets nowhere with it either. Believe me, Laura Lou, I never knew it was in there, and had I known, I would not have paid any attention to it. Read the rest if you care to, and then tear it up and throw it away. Throw it out the window."

She finished reading the letter. "And I can also drive for you, whenever you care to rest."

Edwin chuckled.

"Shall I throw it out the window now?"

"Yes, and tear it into pieces. Let's forget Davera Maloney and never let her let her know we found it. You trust me, don't you dear?"

"Yes."

"Absolutely?"

"Yes, Edwin. I do. I know I do. Doesn't she have a boyfriend?"

"I really couldn't say, but one thing I am sure of is that she is using the wrong tactics this way. At least most fellows wouldn't like it, I'm sure. And now that her letter has gone with the wind, open up the Bible to Hebrews 12:11.

His Bible was beautifully worn from use. It opened easily to the reference. She held her finger at the verse.

"Oh, I know this one. I can quote it without looking. Let's see if we can say it together then."

He caught her hand in his. Her gentle voice blended happily with his deep one.

"Now, no chastening for the present seemeth to be joyous, but grievous: nevertheless afterward it yieldeth the peaceable fruit of righteousness unto them which are exercised thereby."

He smiled down at her. The breeze was blowing her soft hair.

When he spoke, it was with a new balance of judgment and faith in God—and a fresh and deeper richness in his voice. "And we know, Laura Lou, that all things work together for good to those who love the Lord (and we know we do) and to them who are called (and we know we are) 'according to His purpose.' Do you understand? Do you see dear?—and I feel, and I believe I understand the measure of God's great love for us more than I ever did before. We never could have planned all this had we tried ever and ever so hard. Surely these things have come about according to His purpose."

"Edwin, it makes me supremely happy!"

A Simple Picture

By Christmas Carol Hostetler, age 27, Elkhart, Indiana
Originally published August 31, 1930
in the Youth's Christian Companion

The east-bound Oriental Limited roared through the night over shining rails, speeding past golden wheat fields like a blazing arrow. It was a pleasant summer night, and in one of the coaches sat a young man idly watching the strangers around him. Several times he shifted his position restlessly, or peered through the gathering night at the blurred, flying landscape.

At a glance one would judge the young man to be of exceptionally fine character. The general outline of his face showed him to be a man of determination and pluck, yet there was no hint of roughness. He was well dressed, but not according to dictates of the clothiers of the day.

He looked again over the front page of the *Minneapolis Tribune* and laid it beside him mechanically. A tiny speck of white, the corner of something in the crevice of the red plush cushioned seat, caught his eye, and as mechanically as he had discarded the evening paper he drew out the— but instead of finding what he supposed to be a card, he looked straight into the pleasant, half smiling, half plaintive face of a girl. Neil Godfrey frowned slightly, then start in dumb bewilderment. Once he almost laughed, and was about to stick it back in its hiding place, but something with held his hand.

The girl had on a white dress that fell in soft folds around her slender ankles, and she was standing in front of a blossoming dogwood tree. That was all. There was nothing about the picture that would leave the impression she was of high birth or low, her face was intelligent and expressive, her dress neat and dainty, and her position stately, but not haughty. For half an hour he studied her.

Neil wondered at himself that an ordinary picture could claim his undivided attention so long. In fact he was almost disgusted that he was allowing his thoughts, when instead of entertaining a new puzzle, or spending the entire evening watching the people leaving and entering the train, he should be going over his conference speech.

The annual Iowa-Nebraska Conference was scheduled to open session the following day. Neil Godfrey was assigned the subject of "Simplicity," under the general topic of Young Peoples' Problems, to be discussed the second day. His out-line had been definitely decided upon a week before, and two days before leaving home, all the minor points had been filled in. He had spent hours of conscientious study on the subject, and yet he intended to go over it once more on the train, fasten his points, arouse a greater enthusiasm, and readjust a few statements.

Nevertheless, the first hundred miles of a train ride, after a morning of hard work in the field, is not particularly conducive to sound thinking, especially when the little girl across the aisle is tormenting her mother most of the time for ice cream cones or candy, and when half a dozen giddy High School girls just ahead are trying to entertain the entire coach.

Neil still held the picture in his hand. He seemed to have forgotten the laughter and silly performances ahead. Even the child's whines at his side made no effect on him. The expression on the face seemed to change slightly as the light fell on it from different angles. There was something about the face which invited his confidence. It seemed to sympathize, understand, and encourage. Without knowing why, that face seemed to breathe a divine fire within the young man which animated his whole being with desire to be better than he had ever been, to forget the failures he had made, and hope harder, and strive more faithfully. He looked, and the lips seemed to part slightly into a pleasant smile. They seemed almost to speak. "I wonder how her voice sounds?" he said to himself. "Old-fashioned I suppose, like the rest of her."

Just then it occurred to Neil for the first time that her dress was not of the present vogue, though of fashionable length, for the sleeves were gathered at the top and the hem line was decidedly even.

"Oh, mysterious being," he whispered. "Who are you? You look like a woman, but your face is so young, and innocent, so pure, so, so simple. That's it!"

From a brief-case at his right, Neil Godfrey drew out his notebook and jotted something down. Without any difficulty he went over his speech. A new vigor and earnestness spurred him on. An unseen Spirit dominated every thought. He prayed. He closed his note book, put the picture in his inside coat pocket and lay back in his seat for the night.

Neil had nearly finished his speech. The audience had given him splendid attention, and even though the day was hot, they forgot to use their fans. People were leaning forward in their seats. Now and then a hearty "Amen" was given by some of the older men.

"True simplicity is a jewel rarely found," continued Neil. "In character, in manner, in style—the supreme excellence of beauty is simplicity. I had rather a unique coincidence on my trip down here day before yesterday. I found in the seat on the train a small picture of a young woman. Someone evidently lost a treasure, for she is some one's daughter or sweetheart or sister. I was surprised to find such a picture in a public place where all about me seemed saturated with pride and affection, for the longer I looked at that picture of simplicity such as I would wish in a sister of mine if I had one. I would help to solve the problems of the young people, especially of the young men, if our country, yes our church, had more simple, humble, and truehearted young women." Another "Amen" was heard and Neil took his seat.

During the lunch hour that evening someone touched Neil on the shoulder, "Mr. Godfrey?" Neil turned and took the outstretched hand. "Hager is my name," said the tall friendly young chap.

"I'm glad to meet you," said Neil.

"Do you happen to have that picture with you, you spoke of this afternoon?"

"Yes," answered Neil with surprise. And he drew it from his inside coat pocket. The other took it with an utterance of joy.

"I've carried this picture in my Bible for ten years, but I didn't know where I lost it. I remember I had it on the train Tuesday and I moved up a coach to get away from those silly High School girls, and that evening I missed it."

"Your—your lady friend?" stammered Neil blushing slightly.

"Yes, my Mother." Bert Hager noticed the look of astonishment and went on.

"I never saw her. She died when I was about two, and my father gave me this picture when I was eight and I've carried it with me ever since. I've worked for her, lived for her. I'll do anything to please her. She's meant to me what you said today and more. She speaks to me, she loves me, and not every one else does." Bert's voice was a trifle unsteady. He put the picture in his inside coat pocket, tenderly, carefully, as though it might crumble or break.

"I thank you a thousand times. Strange you got the same seat."

"Stranger yet that I noticed it, and stranger still that we met, more than I can tell. I never knew my mother either, and I never saw a picture of her."

"Your father must have one somewhere."

"I never saw it if he has. My step-mother is all right, but she can't understand a fellow like your own. Let me look at her once more."

"Where are you going for the night?" asked Neil after a moment.

"I don't know yet," said Bert.

"Let's go to the same place if you don't mind. I have some problems I'd like to talk over with you. I believe we could understand each other."

"Good," said Bert. They walked to the ticket stand together.

"Your home?" asked Neil.

"Benton, Montana. And yours?"

"Blue River, Washington, and we came on the same train and only found it out? Strange isn't it?"

And in the years to come each discovered many things in the other which helped them solve their peculiar problems, for the prayers of the mothers now in heaven, welded a true and lasting friendship between their boys they left behind.

Hesston, Kansas

Adopted

By Carol Hostetler Kauffman, age 29, Hannibal, Missouri
Originally published March 2 and 9
In the Youth's Christian Companion

It was cold. The wind howled and swirled through the trees at the side of the house, whipping the bare twigs against the window pane every now and then, like some angry unseen spirit.

Agnes looked up nervously and scowled slightly. It was getting cold in the house too. She pinned back a stubborn strand of black hair, and moved her chair a little closer to the table. In a few minutes she had the seventeenth invitation tinted, then placed it beside the other sixteen. After adjusting her chair very carefully, she looked once more over the list of names before her, and began addressing envelopes. The front door opened, but Agnes did not look up nor speak to the boy who blundered across the room.

"Oh, Rich—" Agnes screamed at the top of her voice, and the pen she held in her hand fell on the half-addressed envelope, leaving a blotch of ink on the lower corner, and on the table cloth as well. She turned on her brother indignantly.

"Richard Stern!" she snapped, and the strand of hair fell over her face. "How dare you? You mean old thing! Look there what you made me do." She stamped her foot on the floor. "Laugh, will you?

"I don't see anything funny at that. Keep your cold hands in your pockets where they belong. It's cold enough in here."

Richard only grinned. "You think it's smart to be tormenting some- one all the time. I just wish Annabelle would come walking in some time and see how nasty you act around home, so I do! Did you get your manners at the Ten-cent Store, six for a nickel?"

"And did you get that temper of yours at the Blacksmith Shop—just off the iron?" retorted the boy sarcastically. "I wish Tom Smith would come sometime and hear you spouting off at me. He wouldn't think you were such a sugar-lump."

"Oh, be still. He'd think you were cruel for ramming your icy hands down my back, so there!"

"Agnes," Mrs. Stern stepped in from the direction of the kitchen and spoke in a low voice while she tied on her apron. "Are you quarreling again?"

"It takes two to quarrel, if I know anything! Look there, Mama, at what he made me do on your good table cloth and that envelope is simply ruined. He deserves a good bawling out, and if you don't give it to him, I'll see that he gets it. I might catch my death of cold. He thinks he can just—"

"There, there, Agnes. When Richard learns to behave himself, it won't be hard to control my temper."

"Richard," spoke the woman stepping close to the boy. "You'll soon be a man, and I hope you'll soon learn to act like one. Go down and look at the fire, and bring up a few sweet potatoes."

Mrs. Stern put her hand on the girl's shoulder and looked at the invitations spread out on the table.

"They look very nice, Agnes. I think you can erase that ink spot. Are these the names you've decided on?" She picked up the card and looked at it a moment.

And you're not going to invite Annabell Tison?" she asked.

"No, I am not."

"Here's your spuds, Mama. Where do you want them?"

"In the sink, Richard."

"But she's in your class, Agnes" continued Mrs. Stern. "She'll feel slighted if you don't have her."

"Who's that?" demanded Richard from the kitchen.

"Never mind," returned Agnes. "This is my birthday party and I guess I can invite who I please."

"But what have you against her?" reasoned the mother gently.

"Well, who is she anyway? Nothing but an adopted. She don't even know where she came from. Tisons found her in a drifting boat out on Blue Lake when they went fishing. She was just a skinny little baby and they took her home and raised her and adopted her. She thinks she can run around with all us other girls who come from good homes and know who our parents are."

"But she's just as nice a girl as any in your class," put in Richard. His face was flushed, and he fumbled with his jackknife.

"Of course you'd think so," flashed Agnes; "you seem to see something very charming about the young lady."

Richard did not answer, but it wasn't because he couldn't think of anything to say.

"I wish you would march out of the dining room," she continued; "or keep your suggestions to yourself. I want to get these ready to hand out after Sunday School tomorrow."

"And you're honestly not going to invite Annabelle Tison?" Both mother and brother asked the question at the same time.

"I don't intent do." Said Agnes positively.

"I should think you'd be more particular about my associates. I'm sure if I were her, I wouldn't expect to be invited everywhere. I should think she'd prefer to say at home."

"I'm sorry to hear you talk so, Agnes," spoke Mrs. Stern. "It's the character of your associates I'm particular about. As far as I know she's a good girl and a sincere Christian, too. I've known for a long time she's only an adopted daughter; in fact, I remember when they found her, but Mrs. Tison loves Annabelle as her own, and Annabelle loves Mrs. Tison as much as any girl loves her mother. She's helpful and obedient, and who knows but what her parents were fine people, finer than Tisons? At least we must give Annabelle credit for being what she is."

"I'll say," broke in Richard. "She's the prettiest girl in—"

"Keep still there," snapped Agnes. "You can invite her to your birthday party if you like."

No one ate very much at the evening meal. Richard gulped down a few bites and asked to be excused. Mrs. Stern drank two cups of coffee and munched part of a cinnamon roll. No one touched the sweet potatoes nor the sliced veal, and they looked so delicious. Agnes said the bread was too brown, and the cherries were much too sour, and she didn't like to add sugar to her fruit, so she let them stand.

Mrs. Stern looked hurt and disturbed. She and Mrs. Tison had been fast friends for years. But for a greater reason than that, she wiped away some tears as she washed the dishes alone. She went to her bedroom unusually early and called Mr. Stern. It was unusually late before they went to sleep.

Annabelle Tison did not understand at first what all the whispering was about after Sunday School the next day. Before evening, however, she learned that Agnes Stern was giving a party the next Thursday in honor of her eighteenth birthday, and had given out hand-tinted invitations to all the other girls in the class, and to several of the boys. She was also very conscious of the fact that she had not received one of hers.

* * *

"What is it Annabelle?" The girl's mother looked up from the paper she had been trying to read after church that evening. Something was troubling Annabelle, she felt sure, but it was not the girl's way to express her troubles quickly.

"Oh, nothing, mother." But the girls voice was unsteady and she turned her face to the wall.

"Come, dear, there's something wrong. Don't you feel well today?" You worked to long and hard in the attic yesterday."

"No, I didn't, Mother. I'm alright. I just can't understand some things."

"None of us can, Annabelle. Did I hurt your feelings or misunderstand you?"

"Oh no, Mother; no, no. You've never done that. I just don't know what Agnes Stern has against me lately. Seems like she treats me colder all the time now." The girl could not finish her sentence for the lump that rose in her throat.

"Don't, honey—it hurts me too, but I don't know why she should treat you so coldly."

"She's having a birthday party on Thursday and I'm the only one in the whole class that is not invited."

"NO!"

"Yes, Mother, I—I—"

Annabelle covered her face with her handkerchief and cried softly. "I don't know what I've ever done against her. She tries to turn the other girls against me too. Maybe they hate me because I'm adopted, you know. I heard them whispering something about it once in the cloak room and they didn't know I was standing close and—"

"Annabelle, it's all right." Her mother's voice was so sweet and tender. "You're just as dear to me and—come over here and lay your head on my shoulder. We'll pray about it tonight."

"Oh, Mother, I wish I didn't care so, but—I do; I mean, because I'm not invited."

Thursday dawned bright and fair. The sky was clear and blue, and a warm wind played with the children outside. They ran and laughed and skipped like happy squirrels on a sunny day. It was just the kind of day Agnes hoped it would be. The house was swept and dusted, the porches were scrubbed, the cake was baked and the ice cream was ready to be frozen. Of course several harsh words had been handed out to her mother in the rush of the morning's tasks, but that was nothing unusual. Some mothers were just naturally provoking, you know! Some brothers, too! And of all the days in the year, a girl should have no crosses in her path on her birthday! If folks could only realize how important one's eighteenth birthday is!

And it was even more important than Agnes imagined. It was more than cake and ice cream, games and admiring young friends who would each bring a present she could hardly wait to see.

Agnes did most of the talking at the noon meal. Mr. and Mrs. Stern exchanged glances Agnes could not understand. It made her inquisitive at first, then perplexed. They were such, strange, sympathetic, compassionate glances, somehow apart from things of this world, and now and then their eyes were moist.

"Agnes," spoke her father at last in a gentle faltering voice, as he drew his watch from his pocket. "It's one-fifteen. You may want to go up to your room and close the door. Here is a key," and he drew from his inside vest pocket and old rusty key on a bit of red string, and handed it to the girl. "And at one-twenty-three, you may unlock the object which is standing in the center of your room. It would not have been our way, but you will soon understand."

"What in the world?" asked Agnes quickly as she held out her hand for the key. She wanted to laugh, but it didn't come.

"Ask no more questions, Agnes, but go up and do as I told you."

An uncanny feeling she could not explain seized Agnes as she started up the stairs. She had half a notion to ask her mother to go along. Her mother had gone into the bedroom and had closed the door.

At the head of the stairs Agnes came to an abrupt stop while a baffled look crossed her face. In the center of her room was a small old fashioned trunk. She looked at her watch, and at exactly one-twenty-three, she knelt before the trunk. Very cautiously and with a strange wondering, she turned the rusted lock. The lid cracked and creaked as she tilted it back on its hinges. A more intensely baffled look grew on her face as she stared at its contents. On the top was a white silk dress, yellowed with age, and beside it the picture of a young woman holding a tiny baby. In the other corner on top of an old-fashioned shawl, lay a letter on which was written, "To Agnes Ilene, my Darling, to be opened on her eighteenth birthday." With nervous fingers Agnes tore open the envelope and read:

Penndale Hospital
January 4, 1911

"My only child, Agnes Ilene:

"The doctors say I have only a few day to live, and I must leave you, little one. A kind woman who found me here and told me the Gospel story has promised to adopt you and care for you as her own, and so I can die in peace. I was a wicked woman and your father died a drunkard, but praise God, this woman will soon be your mother, and has led me to Christ, and I am saved and will soon be with Jesus. I want her to take you because I know she will teach you to love the Lord while you are little. Then you will come to me, my little Agnes, come to be with me in heaven. Oh, it must be beautiful there! Last night I dreamed I saw the angels and heard them singing. You are not very strong, little one, but your eyes are big and bright and your smile is the sweetest I ever saw. This good woman will help you grow strong. Oh, she has been so kind to me. Be obedient to her and love her for all this, little one of mine. She is packing your things in my trunk, and mine in my trunk to give you, when you are eighteen. You are not quite one now. It is my request that no one look inside the trunk until you do, on your eighteenth birthday. It is my request that you do not know you are adopted, until you are old enough to appreciate what your foster parents have done for you. I want nothing to hinder your being a beautiful, pure, Christian woman. My hands shake so I can't write long any more. Mrs. Stern will tell you what else you want to know. God bless her, and God bless you, my little lamb. Soon I will kiss you for the last time. Kiss your good mother often for me. Remember, that I die loving you, so love others for me. Read often from the little Bible in the trunk. It is almost like new. Be a good girl, Agnes, my darling. You are to open the trunk at the hour of my departure.

Your mother,
Barbara Lee Tompkin

Agnes swayed with sickness of soul and fell to her knees beside her bed. It was some time before she arose. As in a dream she groped her way to the open trunk and picked up the picture of her mother—her mother.

Oh mystery, incomprehensible, life and death, what eternity of wonder, of grief and love, filled with tears of joy and pain it brings! God in heaven, oh, all wise Heavenly Father, omniscient and omnipotent are they ways. Young hearts are tender and so is God. Agnes wept; but so did Jesus long ago. Her heart was broken, torn and crushed.

Agnes unfolded the wedding dress carefully. It was handmade and trimmed in rhinestones and lace. The shawl was large and bordered with deep fringe. On it was a slip, "Your Grandmother's shawl." Under this was an ivory comb and mirror, and in a tiny box was a cheap gold colored watch with the name "Barbara" on the back. In the bottom of the little trunk was a beautiful white quilt.

It was three o'clock when Agnes locked the trunk and went downstairs. Her face was white and her eyes swollen. She found her mother by the bay-window sewing the snaps on the dress she intended to wear that evening.

"Mother, I love you. I never-never knew what all you've done for me. I— Oh—"

In a moment they were in each other's arms, Agnes with her head on her mother's breast like a little child. They talked between sobs in the sweetest language of love.

"I'm going to put on my wraps now, Mother, and go over to talk to Annabelle. If she can't forgive me, I won't have the party tonight."

Christmas Is Over

By Christmas Carol Kauffman, age 54, Hannibal, Missouri
Originally published December 26, 1954
In the Youth's Christian Companion

"Christmas is over," remarked one clerk to the other with a heavy sigh, as the floor man walked past them toward the big front doors. "And you know what that means." She fumbled with her gold necklace as her eyes followed the floor man.

"Indeed I do," echoed the other. "Look at the mob out there waiting to rush in here as soon as he opens the doors."

"Of course, Pam. That's the headache about this whole crazy affair, isn't it?"

"You mean, *one* of the headaches!"

"You said it, and the worst one. Look at the pushing, edging, and wedging. Everyone wants to be the first one to exchange that thirty-eight blouse for a thirty-two, and those size six gloves for a six and a half, and those ten and one-half hose for nine, and that blue gown for green because Mam, I just can't wear blue with my complexion. Oh, Pam, they make me so mad. That's all we'll get done all day!"

"Right Goldie. Remember the lecture we all got Christmas Eve. The boss said we're to—" she looked around to see if she could spot him.

"Smile," grinned Pam sarcastically, "like this, Goldie. Look and say 'Of course dear, I'll be more than happy to oblige you, Mam. Any size your heat desires. Here they come. No commission today.'"

"Oh, well, 365 days before—"

"Ought to be 1,365 the way I feel right now. Christmas over, then it's that old inventory."

* * *

"Hurry with that box, Jerry. I can't find it, Mamma. You said it was in the clothes closet and it's not."

"Then look under the bed, dear."

Soon Jerry came carrying a cardboard box nearly as big as himself.

"I wish we didn't have to put them away already."

Mrs. Marshall looked into the innocent uplifted face of her four-year-old and smiled.

"But it's best that we do, dear," came her gentle reply. "You see, we wouldn't want any of these pretty figures to get broken, would we?"

"Oh, no-no!"

"Then we ought to wrap each one separately and put them in the box the way they were when Grandma sent them to you. See, like this, Jerry. You take out some tissue paper and wrap up Mary. Next you wrap up one of the Wise Men while I wrap up Mary. Next you wrap one of the angels, while I wrap Joseph. Let's put the manger scene all away while Bobby is asleep."

"So he can't help?"

"He's too little now. He might drop one. That's why we should put them away. We've had to tell him no, no, for two weeks now, and he can't understand. Christmas is over now and if we put these away until next Christmas, then get them out again, Bobby will be old enough to understand better, and we'll all enjoy them better."

Jerry smiled as his chubby little hands reached for his favorite Wise Man in the green robe and gold tie sash

"I hope someday that I can be a Wise Man."

"Mama."

"Yes dear."

"Why is Christmas over now?"

"Christmas day comes only one time a year, on December 25th.

"But can't we let it come again sooner if we want it to?"

"We can't make that day come any sooner, Jerry, but we can talk about it whenever we want to."

"Goodie! Then it won't ever be over, will it?"

* * *

"Reta."

"Yes?"

"Anybody there?"

"What do you mean Annabelle?"

"I mean, I want to talk to you confidentially. I've been trying to get you on the line for over an hour."

"You have?" Well, go ahead. No one is here but Grandpa, and he's deaf, you know. Mother and Betty went to town and Tom is in the basement right now."

"Well, this is Reta. You know that bead bag I worked so hard on last year?"

"Yes."

"Guess what?"

"I haven't the slightest idea, Annabelle. You gave it to Maxine, didn't you?"

"I certainly did. I spent hours and hours on that thing. I took out and put in and worked late into the night on it."

"Well, what of that? What do you mean?"

"Believe it or not, Reta, I got it back yesterday."

"Got it back? You mean to tell me that Maxine gave it back to you?"

"No, that wouldn't have hurt me as much as this did. I just simply can't get over it. Ramona Kastill gave it to me all done up as nice as you please in a silver box and fancy ribbon."

"Oh no!"

"Yes, that very bead bag I made for Maxine. That bag with purple lining. That could mean only one thing, Reta. Maxine gave it to Ramona, and that could mean only one thing too."

"What's that?"

"I can't believe it, she didn't appreciate what I gave her. And I even went to the pains to ask Art if he could tell me something Maxine would like to receive. I'll never use it. Reta, I'll grant you that. Did you ever have such a thing happen to you?

"Don't believe I did, Annabelle.

"Well, Christmas is over and I am just sick!"

"But Annabelle, wait—wait just a minute. Here comes Maxine this very minute and—and Ramona is with her. And Annabelle—are you there?"

"Yes."

"It's this, Annabelle. Ramona is carrying a bead bag. So is Maxine. I'll call you later. Bye."

The cellar door opened and Tom appeared, combing his hair. "May we use the dining room table, Reta?"

"For what? And who's we?"

"I asked Ramona and Maxine to come over. They're going to teach me how to make a bead bag."

"For Martha's birthday?"

"Sure thing. Wouldn't she like that?"

"I would think so."

"I might have to get you to line it for me. I think they're pretty and different. Maxine said her friend gave her hers last year. She made one just like it for Ramona for graduation."

"Then," explained Reta, "Ramona made one just like it for Annabelle. So there!"

"Come ladies," called Tom politely. "Take off your wraps and I'll be right with you. Christmas is over, but I am still in the spirit of making something pretty."

"For a pretty lady," chimed both girls.

"Oh, to be sure," Tom answered.

"It's just like this Myron," said his father, placing one arm around his young son's shoulder. "I'm sorry about that bicycle deal. But I think you understand." He cleared his throat.

"I– I– yes, Dad," Myron looked at the floor.

I had hoped you would, Son. I thought you would, even though it's gone like this for three years now, three Christmases."

Myron bit his lips to keep back the tears. The man tightened his grip on the boy's shoulder.

"When Mother gets out of the hospital–" he reached in his pocket for his handkerchief.

Myron drew a deep breath. "Will she ever Dad?"

"Let's believe it until–Myron, the doctor told me yesterday by next Christmas she ought to be home again."

"Next Christmas!" exclaimed Myron. "You–you mean until?"

It's something to look forward to, Son. Hold on Myron. Let's have faith together. We'll pray like we have never prayed before and believe in our hearts that with God, all things are possible. You don't have any idea how often I see a bicycle for you when I pray. And I intend to get one for you, too."

"I was once a boy, Myron, but I never got my bicycle."

Myron looked up into his father's face searchingly. "Never, Dad?"

The lad's father tightened his grip. "All the more reason why I want you to have one."

Myron pondered. "Well, if Mother can only come home, I won't mind if the fellows do torment me."

"About what, son? You never told me." Myron's eyes filled with tears. "They say I am the son of a no-good-promise father. And now they call me 'bicycle-less Myron' again, like after Christmas," but the lad looked up sharply. "Don't let it make you feel bad. They–they don't understand. Christmas is over and they'll all be telling what they got and–"

"And Myron, we'll begin right away to work and live and pray and plan for next Christmas; what say son?"

"Sure. Look Dad, a man is coming up the steps." Father opened the door.

"Special Delivery for Myron D. Matson."

"For me?" exclaimed Myron.

"If that's your name, son."

Myron tore open the letter. Something blue fell on the floor. "Dear Myron, "I realize your Father has been having an extra heavy load with your mother in the hospital for so long. I visited her last week and she told me that she was very sorry that your father couldn't get you the bicycle you've been wanting; so I am sending you a money order of fifty dollars to get you one. Sorry it's a little late. With love, your Aunt Ellen.

For a moment neither spoke, then—

"Come, Myron," said his father with a voice a little unsteady. "Let's hurry down to Mack's Supply Shop. Mack told me when Christmas is over, he'd have a few bicycles at big reductions."

Myron looked at the calendar to make sure. "And this is the day after, isn't it? Let's go see."

* * *

Suddenly the woman in the hospital bed raised herself on one elbow to speak to the woman in the other bed. "And do you know how to make that pretty popcorn stitch? It's my favorite. I think it is perfectly beautiful. That's what I got down over. I made three bedspreads this past year for my three married nieces, besides two 60 by 90 tablecloths with napkins to match. I combined the hob-knob and half popcorn stitch for that."

"Napkins?"

"A dozen to go with each tablecloth. I'm telling you I worked day and night the past two months to get them done for Christmas. Didn't even take time to go to the table to eat, and when I went to bed I was so tense I couldn't sleep; so I'd get up and crochet some more." She chuckled nervously. "My husband got so peeved with me, it was outrageous how he acted. He said he wished crochet hooks had never been invented, and that Christmas would come around about once in a decade, and so on and so on. He even said if I didn't slow down, I'd drive him crazy, and myself too. Think of that! The doctor gave me a going over, too. Told me to stay in here for two weeks and just rest and never pick up a crochet hook again. Think of that!

"That sounds like my doctor," said the first woman. "He put me in here for a complete rest! He said my nerves were ready to snap, as if I didn't know it myself. But, I was determined to outdo Sally Bond if it took my very blood. You know Sally Bond, she puts her crochet work up at the fair every year."

"Yes, I know."

"I'll bet those are really pretty napkins."

"They are. I just wish I could show them to you. Jack wouldn't call Doris to bring her set up here. I know he wouldn't. He says she's sick of crocheted tablecloths. I'll never hear the end of them being so expensive, either. He calculates my hospital and doctor bill in on it. Says people who eat off oilcloth are lots happier anyhow. But I know what I'll do. I'll ask the nurse to call Mrs. Boyles to come up to see me, and she'll go over and get Doris' set."

"Be quiet," whispered the other woman. "The nurse, don't let her hear. Go ahead now. She walked past our door. I thought she was coming in. My doctor told her when I came in, not to let a soul mention crocheting to me, but just the same, I want to see those napkins. Christmas is over, but before we know it, it'll be here again and I'm going to make some, you see if I don't."

The east bound greyhound bus stopped at Bramtown. A tall bright-eyed young man got on and took a seat beside a middle-aged, dejected looking man in gray who was staring out the window.

"Good evening, sir," greeted the young man. "Did you have a happy Christmas?" He slapped the man on the knee.

"What you talking about kid?" came the gruff reply. "Who said anyone had a happy Christmas?"

"Well, I certainly did! Had the happiest Christmas in all my life."

"Huh!" snarled his seatmate. "S'pose you mean you went on a long drunk and had a fling with a woman."

"No indeed. Quite the opposite. I have never tasted liquor."

"Don't talk baby-stuff with me. I know better. And all this bosh about Merry Christmas is only rot. That's all, plain rot!"

"Sir," objected the young man, turning to face him now. "Never, sir. You're all wrong. Where did you spend Christmas?"

"I hate the day. I hate the trees, holly, and all this tomfoolery over decorating the towns. Silly, ridiculous, absurd, and—well, curses to all this Christmas racket. It's nothing but 'Cut my throat if you can before I cut yours!' You're a kid yet, green and tender. I've been up and down, back and across this country enough to know what I'm talking about."

"I'm sorry to hear your slant of it, sir."

"Got a wife?" The older man nudged the younger in the ribs.

"No sir, Not yet."

"Got a kid?"

"I said I'm not married,"

"Neither am I, but I got a kid somewhere with her mother."

"You were married once?"

"And sorry to say, yes. The ruined everything. Tore me in two. Stripped me bare. Near killed me.

"Near killed you, you say?"

"Worse than a thousand deaths!"

"I'm sorry, very sorry to hear it sir. I hope I'll never have to experience such as that. The Bible gives me a better outlook."

"You're not going to start preaching a sermon to me right here, I hope," snapped the man.

"Listen sir. My name is Richard Blackstone."

"What's that have to do with it?"

"Nothing really sir, only I felt I should introduce myself before we go any further."

"And I suppose your dad is a well-to-do, sending his beloved son off to some religious school to become another Billy Graham. Am I right?"

"Very wrong sir. I'm the fourth in a family of ten children. We've had to work hard, and skimp, and scratch all of our lives; never knew anything but to watch our pennies. I'm working my way through school, preparing to be a foreign missionary and—" The young man pulled his billfold out of his pocket and opened it. "See this girl?" The man nodded.

"The best and sweetest girl in all the world! Joan is her name. And yesterday she made Christmas the happiest day of my life. She promised to be my wife, and together we intend to give our lives to the service of God. He brought us together because we were both walking in His way. She'll never disappoint or deceive me. Christmas is over for a lot of folks, but not for me sir, because—why—why, what's the matter, mister? Are you sick?"

The man slumped. Color left his lips. He made one faint gasp. Richard Blackstone arose. People looked. A few persons blocked the aisle.

"Better stop a minute and see what we can do for this man," Richard called out to the bus driver.

"Too much Christmas, I'll bet," called out one man.

"Poor fellow," whispered Richard. "He never had a Christmas—not a real one."

* * *

"My stomach screams at the sight of the stuff. Gizzard, liver, and pinfeather hash!" A chorus of rebellious remarks followed. The high school students stood in line outside the cafeteria, reading the menu for the day.

"We'll be getting turkey croquettes, turkey soup, creamed turkey on toast, turkey this, turkey that, turkey hash that makes a rash—all week turkey!"

"Sure, for the Knights of Columbus had a big New Year's banquet and they donated their leftover turkey to the high school deep-freeze."

Miriam seldom entered into the daily cafeteria line lingo, but today she spoke. "My father's boss gave us a twenty-four pound turkey and there're only five in our family. So we invited all the widows of our church to come over to eat."

"Widows? Do tell. How many?"

"Only seventeen could come."

"Of all things. Seventeen widows for Christmas dinner. Oh dear me!"

"But it was fun. It really was. Mother and I had the best time getting everything ready. And you should have seen those dear sweet ladies eat! Christmas is over, but as for me, I'm ready for a week of turkey leftovers. And we're going to plan something like that for Christmas next year.

"Well, I wish the Knights of Columbus would have invited in all the widows in town," shouted one student.

"Let's suggest it for next year," proposed another.

* * *

Albert held his small leather-bound New Testament in both hands, then slipped it into his pajama pocket.

"You like your Testament, don't you?" asked his mother pulling back the covers.

Albert answered with a smile.

"Even though you're not old enough to read it, you'll soon learn."

"I can read John 3:16."

Mother agreed with an understanding heart.

"Want me to show you again?" Albert's Sunday-school teacher had fenced the verse with her red pencil and he kept the page marked with the blue ribbon. The class of five-year-olds had repeated the verse in unison in their Christmas exercise.

Albert carried this most highly prized gift from his teacher in his overall pocket all day, then transferred it to his pajama pocket until he finished his bedtime prayer, when it was carefully tucked under his pillow for the night.

Mother sat on the edge of Albert's bed and he snuggled close in the circle of her arm. Without a mistake, he repeated the verse while his right forefinger underlined the three red-marked lines.

"You know if it wasn't for this verse we never would know such a thing as Christmas," said Mother.

"And you couldn't have this verse without the Testament to put it in, could you?"

"That's true, Albert. This is God's book all about Himself and you."

"About me?"

"Yes, you and all of us."

"Is my name in here?"

"You're one of the who-so-evers, Albert."

"That's what Miss Evans told us, too, but is my name Albert in here?"

"There are many, many places where it means you, dear."

Mother squeezed her little son's hand.

"That's the doorbell. You say your prayer and go to sleep. Now that Christmas is over and you have your very own Testament, we'll talk about good things every day." She kissed him tenderly.

"I'm glad that Christmas is over, aren't you?"

"Yes dear and your Testament will show us how to be glad for every new day."

Once I Wished for A Different Name

By Christmas Carol Kauffman, age 57, Hannibal, Missouri
Originally published In the Youth's Christian Companion

Two years ago, I was asked to speak in a church in Lancaster, Pennsylvania, and give interesting experiences of my trip to Switzerland, where I went to gather material for my book "Not Regina."

When the first speaker of the evening was well through his second page of notes, and I had not arrived, the presiding minister left the platform and hurried to the depot. He scanned the waiting room.

"Please," he said to the young man at the ticket window, "page Christmas Carol Kauffman for me."

The young man's lower jaw dropped.

"Pardon, sir?"

"Page Christmas Carol Kauffman, please. It's very important. She should be here somewhere."

"Chris—" Baffled, the young man frowned. Then he stiffened. "Nothing doin'," he said curtly. "You're not makin' a fool of me."

"Mrs. Christmas Carol Kauffman," repeated the minister. "You mean you—?"

Shaking his head with determination, the young man turned and walked away.

Disappointed and humiliated, the minister tried to figure out, on the way back to the church, who had made the miscue, and how he'd word an explanation to the waiting audience.

In the meantime, I made my safe arrival with a friend by car. I had spent several days about forty miles from Lancaster, gathering material for "Hidden Rainbow." Late that evening, when the minister took me to the depot, the same young man was at the ticket window.

"Meet Christmas Carol Kauffman," announced the minister, his eyes twinkling.

I noticed the young man's shoulders drop suddenly as he stared at me. He fumbled for words, but all he could say was a blunt "No!"

"Do I really look like a Christmas Tree?" I chuckled.

He colored. "You mean that really is your name?"

"Don't apologize," I said quickly. "Just fix me up with a ticket to Hannibal, Missouri." Then I opened my bag and handed him one of my books."

"You don't tell me!" he gasped.

"Sorry, sorry. But I thought he was trying to play a joke on me."

The summer before I started to school I fretted considerably about my name. Carol was alright. That's what everyone called me. But I had been told that the teacher must have my full name, date of birth and etc. and I rebelled.

"Mother, I cried, "why did you call me 'Christmas' in front of Carol?"

"Because you were born on Christmas, Dear."

"But, Mother," I reasoned, "is there anybody named 'Thanksgiving' or 'Easter' or 'Fourth of July?'"

"That's different." Mother insisted.

"But they will call me 'Christmas Tree,' and 'Happy New Year,'" I sobbed. "They will! I am sure they will!"

"I doubt that," came her comforting words, which failed to comfort me.

"You have a pretty name. Don't cry about it."

"Well, I don't think it's pretty," I whimpered. "It's funny and queer and way too strange and different. Grace and Anna and Violet and Pearl have prettier names. Lots prettier."

I noticed a hurt look cross my mother's face. Then she said, as she drew me so close, I could smell the scented starch in her striped bib apron, "Someday I'll tell you why we named you 'Christmas Carol.'" She tenderly stroked my hair.

I looked up. She was smiling away a tear. "When, I whispered, when will you tell me?"

"When you are old enough to understand."

"Can't I know now?"

"Hardly."

"But I'll soon be seven. Is it a real real big reason?"

"Yes dear. A very important reason, too. When you understand all about it, you'll like your name, I'm sure."

"I will?" I asked with 99 percent doubt.

"To my knowledge, no one ever called me 'Christmas Tree,' but many heads turned (whenever the roll was called) to better eye the pupil with the funny name. Inevitably, several snickered. Learn to like such a strange name? How could I? Who likes to be stared and snickered at?"

One Sunday, a very sweet young lady student from Goshen College was our dinner guest. I stood rapt as she played the piano and sang. After she left, my father put his hand on my shoulder and said, "You liked the music didn't you, Carol?" I nodded.

"You must learn to play and sing too, for you are our Christmas song, you know." Then Mother told me the story.

"After Nellie was born I was almost an invalid. When she was a year old, I weighed 87 pounds. For over four years, I had to have someone do all the work. I felt so bad life wasn't worth living. Finally, a new doctor came to town, and we consulted him. He told us that having another baby would likely take my life, but there was a faint possibility, my health might improve. Papa and I talked it over many times and prayed a lot with God.

"You were due to be born the last week of January. We had quite another name picked out for a baby girl. 'Gertrude.' Well, God didn't want your name to be Gertrude either. Papa was often away from home on tour with a men's chorus that he sang in. Nellie and I got very lonesome having Papa gone a lot, so Papa bought us a beautiful canary. He thought it would keep us company. It was guaranteed to sing. But three months went by and that canary never ever sang a single note.

"Nellie was five. Three times she said: 'You know what? God told me last night I would have a baby sister on Christmas Day.' We thought of course that she had a dream.

"Christmas Eve came. Papa, Nellie, and I went to church to hear the children's Christmas program. At six o clock the next morning, you were born, a healthy nine-pound baby girl. As soon as you began to cry, the canary bird started to sing. I thought for a moment, I must be in heaven. Then I heard Papa say, 'We have a beautiful healthy baby girl, Mother, a Christmas baby!' 'Then the name we picked out won't suit,' I said. And Papa agreed. 'It's Christmas morning,' I cried, and the canary bird started to sing when it heard you cry. 'We have a baby girl, Mother. A Christmas baby.' Then I said, 'It's Christmas, and the bird is even happy. Listen to it sing! I have never been so happy. Let's name our baby Christmas Carol! Shall we?' Papa thought for a moment, then kissed me and said, 'There couldn't be a more suitable name. She's our Christmas song.' And do you know what?"

"What?" I asked.

"From that day on I was well and wasn't sick any more. It was like a new beginning for me to live healthy again. You were more than an answer to prayer."

"Oh, Mother," I cried, pressing my lips to her forehead. "I'll never say again that I'd rather have another name." Then I ran over and kissed Papa too.

The Night Before Easter

By Christmas Carol Kauffman age 54, Hannibal, Missouri
Originally published in the Youth's Christian Companion

It was the Saturday before Easter, and the streets of Humgate were full of people laden with packages, bundles, boxes of all shapes, sizes, and descriptions. Some were hurrying to catch a bus going south, west or north, while others were hurrying because it was cold. A wet, sticky snow had fallen early that morning, but by noon the temperature had dropped far below the forecast. The snow squeaked when stepped on.

Luther Gathered up his shoeshine box, and started walking west in the biting teeth of the bitter wind. He felt the two cold dimes in his trouser pocket. Twenty cents. His shoulders slumped. That wouldn't even buy a loaf of day-old bread and two dried fish. Dried fish. Luther shrank.

Moving on closer to the buildings, still clutching the two pieces of money, dismal thoughts tormented him. Aunt Sofia had told Luther emphatically not to come home with less that a dollar and a half, for she was tired of nothing but stale bread and fish. As if Luther wasn't!

"Now, Luther," Aunt Sofia had said in her shrill, overbearing voice Luther could not get used to, "now you get yourself down there on Main Street and fetch home some hot cross buns an' real meat for our Easter breakfast. I've 'bout forgotten what meat tastes like. Go now Luther!"

"Yes, Aunt Sofia" returned her nephew. "I'll do my best, but it's awful cold, and you know when it's this cold, folks—"

"Cold or no cold!" broke in the commanding voice, "we've got to have a decent meal once."

Pallid and fearful, Luther turned up the collar on his brown tattered jacket, and started toward the door. He felt distinctly forlorn, sad and lonely, lonelier than ever before in his life. Luther was small fourteen.

For the past eight months, the boy had been staying with his father's only sister, Sofia, solely because before his father's passing, he had requested that Sofia give Luther, his orphaned son, a good respectable home. The thrill of expectance of finding his aunt's home in Hungate a pleasant and happy abode, was soon turned into a stark reality quite the opposite. Disappointed, the boy lay down on his hard single bed night after night, torn by exploded dreams of Aunt Sofia's kindness, restless with pent-up emotions and longings and vague but happy memories of his real mother and love. Luther had repeatedly cried out under the covers, blindly, brokenheartedly, sometimes stupefied with an unnatural exhaustion. Luther was thin, sad, and very tired. He told himself, "I have only a jammed up boy's life."

Why was he left an orphan? But worse, why did Father request Aunt Sofia to take him? Happy home indeed! Good home! Night after night Luther had babbled, cried, and groaned alone is his dingy dismal room.

Aunt Sofia never guessed the boy's anguish, at least she never showed any signs of concern. But with each new morning, Luther determined afresh to try his best to please the seventy-year-old woman who was not a whit like his father. Indeed she was almost repulsive now always complaining, always stern, always unreasonable!

"But, I was out all morning shoveling snow," Luther ventured, his one hand on the door knob.

"And it's even colder now."

"But you brought me only enough to buy fuel for Sunday," Sofia flared. "No arguing out of you now Luther. Be off now and come home with hot cross buns and meat, or I will be mad as a hornet. Yes, I will!"

"But, what if I can't get customers today?"

"I say then, don't come home without. Surely of all days in the year, folks'll want nice shined-up shoes and boots for Easter."

"But those who can afford it will all have new ones."

Luther slipped out. What was the use to try to explain anything to Aunt Sofia or tell her the poor shined their own shoes if they got shined, or that no one would stop on the cold street corner or much less stop to take off their overshoes to have shoes shined on a day like this. And what was the use to try to tell her he would likely catch a dreadful cold standing all afternoon in the bitter cold. Luther learned months ago that Aunt Sofia was not only mean and selfish, but absurd, cruel, and unreasonable. Very likely if he did bring home a dozen hot cross buns and meat, she would eat more than half of it herself as before. Surely Father did not know this part of Aunt Sofia.

Sadly, Luther trudged toward town, mumbling to his own sad self. "No, mother, no father, no brother or sister. No nothing!—But, work for someone who is cross. Might be better off in an orphanage, but I know I'm too old. Those children at least will surely have a good hot dinner tomorrow. Eggs for the Children's Home—I saw that in a newspaper last night. 'Eggs for Easter.' I wish I knew what that is all about."

And Luther was right when he said it would be too cold for folks to stop for a shine. He had stood waiting, watching, expecting, until he was sure his hands and feet would freeze. Hundreds hurried past. No one hesitated. Finally in desperation to get warm, Luther walked three blocks over to the train depot.

A well-dressed man, beginning to gray at the temples, put a hand on the boy's shoulder. "Ready for Easter, my boy?"

"Me?" inquired Luther. "Ready you say? No, sir, not me."

"Why not? It's almost here you know."

"Yes, I know, sir, but well—" Luther shifted from one cold foot to the other, "as for me sir, I wish Easter came in the summertime."

"This is hectic weather for Easter isn't it?" Laughed the gentleman. "There's plenty of humans cussing this nasty weather. Think all the ladies who want to wear their new Easter bonnets tomorrow." He laughed again. "But you son, why do you say what you did? I'm interested."

"Because," Luther swallowed. "it's hard to get customers when there's snow and cold on the streets."

"Customers? Oh, is that your shoeshine outfit you got there?"

"Yes, sir. Need a shine, sir?"

"Sorry son. Just had them shined in the hotel, else I sure would."

The man noticed two shiny tears quiver in the lad's eyes. "But here," he said, drawing change from his deep pocket. "Here, take it anyhow," He put two dimes into Luther's hand. It will buy you a couple of candy bars for your Easter."

And that is how Luther was clutching two cold dimes in his blue cold hand as he was making his way west. The early night was now crowding around him, reminding the day was spent and he had made nothing. The afternoon had been one of almost unbearable long chilling weather; and not a single customer.

Discouraged and frightened, Luther made wild, desperate, deep inside groans as he pushed himself on. The icy wind whipped and stung his face and ears. He passed the city part where beautiful, majestic organ music was heard from a loudspeaker. He stood a moment trembling. It reminded him of music he had heard once when his father had taken him to an organ recital in the Notre Dame Cathedral. He remembered being with his father, and tears came to his eyes. It made him think of the happy days back in Germany years ago.

He could not dare to stop any longer. On, he must go toward the upstairs rooms where Aunt Sofia would be waiting and angry.

In front of a large stone house, sitting well back from the street, Luther paused. From every window, there shone bright lights. He must do something. He found himself walking up to the front door and pressing the doorbell. A man in a freshly ironed shirt and a wine colored jacket, opened the door. Surprise and disgust crossed his smooth shaven face.

"Please sir, are you the master of the house?" asked Luther.

"Sorry, but I thought maybe I could shine yur shoes tonight."

"Ho, ho," sneered the man. "The sooner you run along, the better it will be for you." He closed the door in Luther's face.

Luther left as tears welled up in his eyes. He was almost bitter. He passed more fine homes and could see where people were seated around food covered tables and clustered around warm flame-filled fireplaces. Inside people were eating, laughing, gay, well-dressed and warm. The thin soup he had for lunch was long gone from his empty stomach. Close to the cement walk was a gray frame house, beside an empty lot. In the window, a white candle burned on a table beside a beautiful potted lily. Luther stepped close and put one hand on the window pane. He did not see the child behind the table watching.

"Oh, Mama, cried the little girl, "look at the dirty ragged boy. He's peeking in our window. Make him go away, Mama. He scares me."

The door opened, but Luther was already walking on, bending his body against the piercing wind. "What is this Easter, anyhow?" he asked himself. It makes people push me away. Nobody loves me. I hate Easter. I wish it never was."

The the tracks came to a cross. From there on, the houses were most all dingy and falling apart. It was low rent places for poor class renters. The dingy taverns were all crowded with both men and women hollering and laughing above senseless weird jukebox honky-tonk music.

In the window of a small one-story frame house, the worn lace curtain was pinned back, and on a table, beside a small oil lamp, was an open songbook and two colored pictures, less than a foot square and a small white lamb. Luther put his shoe shine box down on the sidewalk and stood on it to see better. Unnoticed, he stood looking. One picture was a man nailed to a cross of wood, the other man, in a white robe standing in a garden with a woman kneeling before him. In the center of the room, meagerly furnished, Luther saw a young woman rocking close beside a heating stove. On her lap sat a curly haired boy in night clothes and beside her in the circle of her one arm, stood a little girl. The woman was reading out loud from a large black-bound book.

"Read me it once more, Mother," begged the little girl. "And put in my name this time like you did for Bobby. I like the story when you tell it that way, Mother."

"There's but one more stick of wood, dear, the mother replied. "So I'll have to do it quickly, then we'd better hop into bed to keep warm."

"An, the oil in the lamp in the window, too, Mother. See, it's almost—oh, Mother, look, I—oh, I was sure I saw a face at the window, Mother."

"A face, Barbie?"

"Why, yes, Mother. Let's invite him in. It looked like one, you know, Mother, how you said. It looked rejected and oppressed, and afflicted. See, yes, there it is, Mother. Let's invite him in. He must be very cold. Maybe—maybe he's a boy like the boy you read to us about last night, you know, Mother, that found that verse in the Bible the night before Easter day when he got hurt so bad and thought he was going to die."

"We'll see. Go open the door, Barbie dear, and ask him what he wants." The child obeyed.

"Are you—say, are you a wondering boy?" called the child to Luther.

"A what?" asked Luther. "I'm a shoe shine boy, that's all."

"Well, are you hunting around for the wounded and bruised lamb like we have on our table who was nailed to the cross for us?"

"The Lamb?" asked Luther. "I didn't know how anybody's lamb was hurt or lost or anything. I'm hunting for—well, for what this in your window means. No one has ever told me. Is this what Easter means?"

"Come in out of the cold," called the woman. We have a little fire left yet."

"Thanks, thanks," said Luther, stepping gladly close to the stove.

"I've been cold all day. This feels wonderful, wonderful."

"Barbie, push him the stool and put in the stick of wood. Your coat isn't heavy enough for this kind of weather, my boy."

Barbie dear, pour him a cup of tea if it's still warm. You say you're wondering what Easter means and no one has told you? You mean never?"

"No one has ever told me, can you? I'm puzzled."

"The tea is still warm," said Barbie, pouring it, "and he can have my cupcake the teacher gave me at school today. Here it is." She held it out to Luther.

"Sorry it's not more," spoke the mother, "but such as the good Lord has blessed us with, we're willing to share it with you."

"Is it good?" asked Barbie.

"Very, very good. And thanks," answered Luther.

"Tell him quickly Mother, before the fire is out and before the oil is all. The he will be happy too, like the boy in the story was the night before Easter. Listen! What is that, Mother? Someone is singing by our house."

Barbie ran and peeked out the window. "Why, Mother, there's a whole bunch of people singing right outside our door here."

Clear and sweet came the music "Christ who left His home in glory." Luther sat fixed and spellbound. Never had he heard anything like it. "And upon the cross was slain."

Then a gentle knock. "Here is a little something to help make your Easter a bit happier, Mrs. Platt." The first man entered and placed a bushel basket of groceries in the middle of the room. A second followed with another, as big and as full. One young lady carried a red fluffy comforter, another a large dishpan full of fruit.

"What?" cried the woman in tears. "All this? For us?"

"In the name of our risen Lord and Savior, Jesus Christ, Mrs. Platt. We thought that since this is the first Easter since your husband is gone, we'd try to give you a little lift. It's from the "Gifts for Him" class."

"Oh, Mother!" exclaimed Barbie, on both knees beside one of the baskets.

"Potatoes an' bread, real butter, and bacon, eggs, an' look, a really truly chicken, an' noodles. Oh, oh an' cakes, and potato chips an' candy!!"

"This is too good to be true!" cried the excited mother.

The door was opened and in came two more young men carrying great arm fulls of wood.

"The Father, God, and Lord of Lords, bless and reward all of you dear dear good saints," choked the mother through her grateful tears.

"He already has, Mrs. Platt."

"Now you can make more fire an' tell the boy, Mother," explained Barbie in glee.

"Yes dear, I can and will."

When the visitors had all gone, Mrs. Platt began asking the visitor his name. Briefly Luther told his sad, but true story.

"Luther, if you are afraid to go home tonight in the dark, I will fix you a bed here," said Mrs. Platt. "Tomorrow morning while the chicken is cooking, I'll go over and invite your Aunt Sofia to come back and eat dinner with us. How's that?"

"But she won't come, I know. Aunt Sofia never walks far."

"Oh?"

"But, I know," Luther's face lighted up. "I have two dimes. That will bring her over on the bus and take her back again. A man in the depot gave them to me for candy."

"Then you won't have any," ventured the little curly haired boy sympathetically.

"That's all right," answered Luther. "I'd much rather hear what Easter means. But I must bring my shoe shine box inside before I forget it."

"Of course," agreed Mrs. Platte, beaming. "Go bring it inside and before I go to bed, you shall hear the Easter Story, for Christ said, Luther, that if with all your heart ye truly seek me, ye shall ever surely find me. It is in the blessed book, the Bible, the Word of God. Barbie, set the kettle on the stove dear, and we'll all drink tea and eat some of the good, good things together and in the morning after I get back from going over to see your Aunt Sofia, Luther listen, we'll all go to church together, won't we?"

Luther drew a long deep breath and swallowed. "To church?" he gasped. "I've never been there."

"Oh," smiled Mrs. Platt, "but after you've heard the story of what Easter means, you'll want to go every Sunday, your whole life left."

"I will?" asked Luther, wide-eyed with both surprise and doubt.

"You will," agreed Barbie. "Mother is right, you just will. It's all so beautiful." Barbie followed Luther to the door. "An' Mother knows the best ways to tell stories, so you'll understand them better how the Lamb got bruised for our sins. You know, Jesus was a lamb an' with his stripes we got healed, an', the cross, you know, the cross He got nailed to wasn't a bit nice, but they couldn't keep Him in the tomb place either. Mother will tell you all of it when you bring in your shoe shine box now."

Luther smiled like he hadn't smiled in eight months. "For so small a girl, you seem to know an awful lot, Barbie," he said.

"An, bet I know an awful lot Barbie," he said.

"An I bet I know something you don't know," exclaimed Barbie, holding Luther by one hand. "I'm going to get a brand new Bible in Sunday School tomorrow."

"How's that? asked Luther.

"Because I'm going to win you for Christ, tonight. Mother an' me." Her eyes danced. Her cheeks glowed.

Luther stared.

"Go bring it in boy," urged Barbie. "We've been trying all week, haven't we Mother? And now it's the night just before Easter and late as bedtime and he stopped by. Oh, I'm so glad and happy cause I just know he will, and Mother," whispered Barbie, "if that bad old Aunt Sofia won't turn her self around and be nice, maybe he could come and live with us."

"Shush, Barbie dear. We'll see. Brother Bartum might have a better plan. Just wait. It's the night before Easter and this one big thing we must first do, lead him to Christ."

"Yes, Mother," whispered Barbie softly. "We'll win him first."

They Built a Fence

By Christmas Carol Kauffman, age 57, Hannibal, Missouri
Originally published in the Youth's Christian Companion

Keith astonished everyone. You could almost hear your own heart beat when he got up and made his speech, and ended saying, "I suggest we all get together some evening soon, and help build a brand new fence." That's exactly the way he put it.

Silence enveloped the room. Finally Tim Hayworth (after Sally pressed his arm meaningfully) said, "Why don't you put that suggestion in the form of a motion, Keith?"

And did you know it carried? Almost unanimously!

No, it wasn't an all-American white picket fence not a modern stretcher-type, not a slat, not a wire, screen, basket weave, post and rail, louvered, nor any such fence—that Keith Hayworth made reference to. You will too very soon, unless you stop reading.

It seems that Keith was born to be a leader. That is, since he made that tremendous change. Folks have never stopped talking about it. The change.

It stated when Keith quit running around with a chic little redhead teenager he called "Birdie," and began bringing Enga to church. Enga is that sweet, attractive girl Keith's aunt and uncle brought along home with them from the conference in Germany. She had been an orphan but now she had outgrown the orphanage. Everyone in the church, and even outsiders, could see that she was drawing the very best out of Keith. Folks who cared most rejoiced most. And who cared more than his own parents and grandparents? No one! For who had worked more diligently and conscientiously, to keep the fence in repair then they?

This particular fence problem had become a real issue one evening when Keith, in an outburst of vexation, shouted to his father: "Let's do away with the old outdated, dilapidated ideas altogether. I am sick and tired of being fenced in!"

"You mean, no fence at all?" feebly ventured grandfather, rubbing his once sturdy hand, slowly across his bald head.

"Why not?" retorted Keith, without giving Grandfather a glance.

Grandfather hesitated. "Then my boy, we, we soon wouldn't have anything to call our own." Grandfather spoke in a strange quivery voice that was distinctly sad. "Why, Keith, that could mean the ruin of everything your parents, and our forefathers have worked and struggled for, and lived and died for. Don't talk foolishly, my boy." Grandfather swallowed hard. He started to get up, then sat down as though he were very, very tired. "You can't mean what you said, Keith. You just can't."

Keith coughed . "Well, I think we've lived here in this community long enough. I'm ready to move someplace where they don't have these silly fences to keep us in." And with that, Keith dashed upstairs two steps at a time.

Keith did not go out to see Birdie that night. He sat on the edge of his bed with his head resting on the table close beside it. The clock downstairs struck ten, eleven, eleven-thirty before he snapped out the light.

Keith had Enga beside him at the MYF that evening. The guest speaker was a middle-aged minister from Holland. "Oh, I remember him," whispered Enga to Keith. "He visited the orphanage in Germany and spoke to us children. It was the first time I heard God calling my name."

"One thing I notice here in America," said the minister, "are your fences. They interest me much. We do not have so many fences in Holland."

Keith sat up straight.

"We have few fences around our farms, because we have canals. But, sorry to say, the spiritual fences around our churches are too weak and too few. Our church fathers worked hard, and with keen consciences, to set the fence posts in solid rock. You see baptism on one's own confession of faith, nonbearing of arms, non-swearing of oaths, separation from the world in many aspects, simplicity and purity of life mutual love and sharing, and loyalty to the inspired Word of God—these are only some of the spiritual fence posts we cannot afford to more or uproot. Listen to me, dear young people here tonight; you hardly realize, as I do the importance of helping to maintain these Bible teachings and doctrines our forefathers upheld. In many places where I've been, here in America, people seemingly are trying to discard these fences and destroy altogether, every evidence of separation from the world. Should that happen here (but I pray it never will), very soon you too, would lose what is most precious to you, and that which makes you most precious to Him. You see—"

Keith sent a fleeting glance over at Enga. At the same instant she sent a fleeting glance to him.

"You see—"

For forty-five minutes the Dutch minister continued. The story of his conversion, his romance, his ordination, and his interest in young people, held their undiminished attention. He concluded by mentioning again the importance of maintaining the fence.

Then Keith astonished everyone when he got up as soon as the minister sat down.

"Tonight," he said, "I want to confess I've been guilty of trying to destroy our church fence. I'm sorry. I'm ashamed. I'm sure you all got the point of our brother's illustration. Everything he told us tonight is true. For several weeks I've been trying to find the answers to a number of—well, I guess I'll call them 'panels' or 'sections' in our church fence. I wish we as a group here could, or would, invite our parents and ministers to meet with us and discuss very frankly and very freely with each other, how we feel about our ordinances and these Bible doctrines. I mean, ask each other questions. So we'd all know the true and honest 'why' for everything our church stands for. Too many of us consider this fence as our brother so fittingly named it, an antique thing that someone else built to pen us in. I know I've felt that way often.

"If we helped to repair it, or paint it, or reset some posts, or whatever, maybe it wouldn't seem like such an offensive thing. I got an idea while he was speaking . I suggest we all get together sometime soon, and help build a brand new fence. We may decide to build it just like the old one. I don't know. I don't want to be radical. I just want to be fair and sensible and be a booster for what's right."

Three years can bring about a lot of changes. That's what Grandfather says to himself every time his grandson stands behind the pulpit and Enga looks trustingly over the head of her baby boy into the face of her minister husband.

"Keith," inquired a visiting preacher from the south, "how did you build up this fine group of young people in your church?"

"Me? Brother, I didn't" Keith answered. "We got together, young and old, and discussed our fence, then we all helped rebuild it."

"Fence?"

"You don't understand," laughed Keith. "Go along home to dinner with us, and I'll tell you all about it."

Twenty-Seven Years a Contributor

An article by the Youth's Christian Companion *editor*
December 26, 1954, about Christmas Carol Kauffman

Christmas Carol Kauffman has been the longest continuing contributor to the *Youth's Christian Companion*, whom the editor has had. She also has served in a most distinctive manner. She has written more than any one other or possibly a number of regular contributors put together over these years; and she has produced for the editor more book length manuscripts than any other author. Our readers will readily remember her for her numerous serials, that last of which was "Not Regina," which is now for sale in book form. It was therefore, but natural that the editor would invite her to send a testimony, if she were led to do. I wish to thank her for her kindness, and assure her that her services have been greatly appreciated by the readers and the editor. May God bless her in her continued ministry with her gift and make her a mighty spiritual influence in influencing the lives of thousands of young people in the days to come, and through the pages of the *Youth's Christian Companion*.

Christmas Carol's Response

Twenty-seven years ago I received my first letter from Brother C. F. Yake, informing me that a short story which I had written for a class assignment in Literature, while a student at Hesston College, was accepted for publication in the *Youth's Christian Companion*. To be sure, I was pleased, but the next line nearly took me off my feet, for it told me

I had talent to write which should be developed and dedicated to God and the Church.

Talent to write? Stories? Me? Surely the letter had been mis-sent. Looking at the envelope once more, I began all over. I held my breath, for the concluding paragraph asked if I would agree to send him a short story a month!

From that day to this, Brother Yake has been a friend, a special friend, a brother, a church father of inestimable inspiration to me. He made me feel somehow that we must be workers together in one great united effort, to save our growing young people from the world and for God and the Church. Without such a relationship between editor and contributor, writing stories, at least for me, would have ceased long ago.

So I wish to take this opportunity to thank Brother Yake personally, for his many kindnesses, considerations, encouragements, corrections and counseling, with Christian loyalties in all circumstances down through these twenty-seven years. It has been a pleasure to work with this man whose returning prayer from his office is that God will bless the new editor and continue to enrich the lives of our youth in the pages of the *Youth's Christian Companion*. The many letters in my files from his pen indicate that his heart and soul has been in his work. My own heartfelt prayer is that God will use me to help carry out Brother Yake's hopes and desires in this means of witnessing for our Lord and Master Jesus Christ.

Christmas Carol Kauffman

You Don't Fit In

By Christmas Carol Kauffman, age 49, Hannibal, Missouri
Originally published March 15, 1953
In the Youth's Christian Companion

Janet stood outside the classroom door, waiting.

"Here Mel," she whispered, slipping a tightly folded note into Melva's hand. "Read it quickly before class takes up."

Melva walked to the rear of the classroom, put her books down on the window sill and unfolded the note.

"Please, Mel," she read, "be a good sport. Please give me 100 on the exam, and I'll do the same for you in case I miss any. I'll thank you the rest of my days—and I will explain why later. I'm not prepared for today."

Melva folded the paper and stuck it deep into her sweater pocket. For a moment she remained at the window looking across the beautiful campus.

"Janet will explain," she said to herself. "Well, she never seems to be prepared for the weekly exams. Not prepared today. Explain later."

Melva took her seat; Janet the one to her immediate left. Janet cast Melva a sidewise glance and winked. Melva did not answer the wink, but opened her history book and scanned the assignment.

"Books closed," announced Mr. Blake. "You may answer the next 25 questions true or false."

Janet looked up into the young teacher's face and smiled.

"Ready. Number one."

When the test was finished, papers were exchanged left to right across the room. The teacher red correct answers, checking was made and papers returned.

At the top of Melva's paper, Janet had marked a bold 100. Melva returned Janet's paper without a grade, but with six answers checked wrong. Janet's cheeks got red. Her lips tightened. At the close of the class period, she was first to leave the room.

Near the end of the hall, she waited for Melva. She grabbed her by the arm and pulled her aside.

"Didn't you read my note?" she asked in an exasperated tone.

"Yes, I did."

"Then why didn't you help me out? I gave you a hundred and you missed three."

"You shouldn't have done it Janet. It's not right!"

"Shoot! Plenty of other students do it all the time."

"But Janet, I never was used to—"

"Oh, Melva, you are always such a goody-goody student. You surely don't fit in at all! At least with this school gang here. You really make me mad!"

"I'd be at one of our church schools this year if my father would not have died. I know I don't fit in here, but—"

"And they don't help each other out at your church school?"

"Yes, indeed they do help each other out, Janet, but not in—I mean, I hope none of them help each other out by being dishonest."

"So you call me dishonest, do you, just because I was trying to be real nice and kind to you?"

"I'm going to have my seat changed, miss goody-two-shoes!" Janet hurried down the hall.

Melva went directly to the study hall and opened her Latin book, but it was too difficult to concentrate. "You don't fit in." Janet's comment repeated itself over and over in her mind.

After lunch, she knocked on Mr. Blake's door. "Come in and take a seat." He pointed to a chair.

"I came in to speak to you about my test paper."

"Which test paper?"

"The true and false test you gave us this morning."

"Yes, I noticed you made 100 on yours."

The teacher pushed his chair closer to his desk, looked through the stack of papers and drew out the right one.

"But I did not deserve 100," Melva answered. "I missed three. The girl who graded it made a mistake."

"Let me check to make sure." With a pencil Mr. Blake went down the list of answers. "Yes, five is wrong, and number nine, and number seventeen. You are right. You missed three. Who marked your paper?"

"Janet, but I did not come to report her mistake, you understand, I only came to report that I do not deserve a 100. You should change the grade on your record."

"I must say, I admire your honesty." He moved his swivel chair back. "Would you care to tell me just why you came in to make this correction?"

"Well, I have a conscience against being dishonest; that's why. Maybe some would call it a little thing, but—" Melva rubbed the palm of her hand across the notebook. "Father always taught us children it is wrong to cheat."

"Is your father a minister, Melva?"

"My father is not living. No, he wasn't a minister, but he was a real, true Christian. I— I really wanted to go to a Christian school close by, but after he passed away, I knew Mother would not have the money to send me.

"Is it hard to be a Christian here in this school?"

"Sometimes. I realize I don't fit in very well here." She hesitated. "I suppose it would be harder if I didn't go home every night. That helps."

The teacher sat thinking. "This is the first time in my three years of teaching here at the school, that a pupil has come in to ask me to lower a grade. The faculty met together last evening to discuss having some talks, given by students in our next assembly, about better conduct in the classroom. We need something like that here for sure. Would you be willing to give us a talk sometime about being honest?"

Melva felt her cheeks getting warm. She drew a very long deep breath.

"Tell, for instance, how it is possible for a classmate to make a mistake in grading a paper?" he suggested.

"Yes, but—"

"I think you could do it Melva."

The door opened. Had someone knocked?

"It's better to have a student tell something out of his own experience," continued Mr. Blake, "than for one of us to give a lecture. There's entirely too much dishonesty going on here in school; we all know that. Think it over, Melva and let me know in a day or so."

"Yes, Miss Grant?" The teacher shifted his glance and addressed the teacher at the door.

Janet was standing outside in the hall. She pulled Melva into the cloakroom.

"You told him?" she asked with much anger.

"I told him to change my grade."

"And, what about my grade?"

"I never mentioned your grade."

"You told him about my note?"

"No, Janet, I never mentioned the note,"

"I don't believe you! I heard what he was saying to you when Miss Grant opened the door."

"Truly Janet, I did not tell on you. I do not intend to either. You can tell him that yourself if you like."

"Why did you tell him to change your grade? Oh, I could just shake you, Melva!"

"Janet, don't be angry. Walk home with me. We can't talk here."

"I'm going to a basketball game."

"Maybe I could see you tomorrow sometime then?"

"Well, Melva, I'll be honest with you right now. You're just not my kind, and I can't believe that you didn't tattle to Mr. Blake about me. Did you give him the note I gave you?"

"No, here it is." Melva reached for it in her sweater. Janet took it and hurried out the room and down the steps.

After Melva read her Bible that evening, she knelt as usual beside her bed to pray. "Dear Lord Jesus, help me to prepare the talk and give it in such a way that Janet will know that I am not trying to be pious, but I must be honest."

A week passed and Janet went out of her way to avoid Melva.

"Mother," said Melva one evening with tears, "I fit into that high school crowd less all the time. I can hardly wait until the term is over."

"You wouldn't want to fit in, would you?"

"No, of course not!" But if I could only find one friend who believes like I do. It's so hard to always be alone, Mother!"

"I know dear, but when only one light shines, just think how dark it would be if that one went out."

"I'm to give a talk in assembly tomorrow, and I know before I give it, what most of the students will think!"

"No, Melva, don't say it, dear. I know how you must feel, but think how happy Father would be if he knew you were the one chosen to give it."

"Just be yourself. I will be praying for you."

The students and faculty sat quietly. It wasn't a flowery speech with dramatic gestures. In simple vocabulary, but with an honest conviction that made her forget herself, Melva talked confidently on "The Principal and Rewards of Honesty." But only a few clapped. Evidently her talk had been a flop. Sadly she left the platform and hurried to the cloakroom. She wanted to be alone. She just didn't fit into the crowd.

The door opened. "Melva," she felt an arm around her shoulders. It was Janet. "May I go home with you tonight?"

"With me?" Of course you may!"

"I'd like for you to tell me that talk all over again."

"The one I just gave?"

"Yes."

"But it was a flop!"

"No, it wasn't a flop. It was so good no one felt like clapping. It hit almost everyone of us. Everybody can see you had something so good to say. Oh, Melva, you just don't fit in here at all, but I know I fit in too well, and I'm miserable. I must go now, but I'll see you later tonight."